AUTHOR	CLASS
ROBERTS, L	F

TITLE   Not enough horses

Not Enough Horses

When an acquaintance of Saxon's, bit actor and part-time male prostitute, Robbie Bingham, dies in a mysterious car explosion and the police don't seem to care, Saxon goes into action.

He pokes around the netherworld of dimly lit gay bars of West Hollywood and the boardrooms of a television network, and along the way runs afoul of a vindictive pimp, a pompous game-show host, a cadre of venal and frightened TV executives, an ice-cold Beverly Hills homocide detective, and a movie sex goddess who is fighting the encroachment of years with straight bourbon and a lover twenty years her junior. Saxon's investigation leads him in two directions at once, and climaxes with a sudden and fiery death. And then there is Marvel – one of the 'lost children' of Hollywood, who survives on the streets, retains the innocence of childhood, and makes sure Saxon will never look at things in quite the same way again.

Les Roberts' first novel, *An Infinite Number of Monkeys*, won the Best First Private Eye Novel Competition run in conjunction with the Private Eye Writers of America. *Not Enough Horses* is a splendid and worthy successor.

Not Enough Horses

Les Roberts

MACMILLAN
LONDON

Copyright © 1988 by Les Roberts

First published in the United States of America

First published in the United Kingdom 1988 by
MACMILLAN LONDON LIMITED
4 Little Essex Street London WC2R 3LF
and Basingstoke

Associated companies in Auckland, Delhi, Dublin, Gaborone,
Hamburg, Harare, Hong Kong, Johannesburg, Kuala Lumpur,
Lagos, Manzini, Melbourne, Mexico City, Nairobi, New York,
Singapore and Tokyo

British Library Cataloguing in Publication Data

Roberts, Les
  Not enough horses.
  I. Title
  813'.54[F]

ISBN 0-333-47348-5

Printed and bound in England
by Richard Clay Ltd, Chichester, Sussex

For Gail, Valerie and Darren –
the Constant Three . . .

1

He was slim as a reed, graceful as a willow, and gay as a springtime gambol through the woods. When I shook his hand his skin was smooth and cool, and the handshake was definite without being firm. He sat down in the chair opposite my desk and didn't cross his legs so much as wind one around the other. His hair was blond, except at the roots, and in the bright California sunlight coming through the window it was obvious he was wearing makeup. He wore a boat-necked electric-blue blouse that exposed the dark hair on his forearms and a pair of ultratight faded jeans. His eyes were almost as blue as the blouse. His long hands fluttered about his face nervously for a few moments, and then he calmed them by clasping them on his right knee, which rested on his left one.

"Mr. Saxon," he said, "I'm a friend of Robbie Bingham." He left that hanging, waiting for a reaction. The name sounded familiar, but I couldn't place it or put a face to it and said so.

"Robbie worked with you on a picture, about six or eight months ago. *The Calico Cat;* was that the name of it?" The young man, whose name was Kevin Brody, took a wallet from his leather purse and reached across the desk to show me a photograph of a very handsome boy-man, and all at once the connection kicked in.

"Oh, sure. Robbie. I guess we never got around to last names."

"Robbie was fascinated by you," Kevin said. "An actor who works as a private detective."

"More like a PI who occasionally works as an actor. I'd like it to be the other way around."

"Robbie said most of the actors treated the extras like dog shit, but that you were very nice to him."

I recalled Robbie Bingham as a beautiful young man with a great sense of humor and an almost puppylike hero worship of anyone who actually had lines to speak on the film. He'd admitted to me on the first day that he was gay but told me not to worry because I was too old for him, and I told him I was used to rejection, and we laughed, and then he'd hung around me for the two weeks he was on the set. I had never really encouraged him, but I never cut him either, because he had that rare knack of making people laugh at his seeming naïveté. He also had a fierce determination to make it as an actor. I had enjoyed his company.

"That was nice of him to say," I said. "We had a good time together. How is he, anyway?"

Kevin looked shocked, incredulous. "You don't know?" he said, as though whatever there was to know I should have heard about. Then, "Robbie is dead. He was murdered."

That was a conversation stopper, no doubt about it. I finally said, "God, I'm so sorry."

"You didn't read it in the newspapers?"

"I've been away for over two weeks, up in the wine country, getting a little smog-free air." I realized Kevin Brody did not want to hear about how I spent my summer vacation. "How did it happen?"

Kevin's eyes filled with tears and became red-rimmed. His mascara ran a little bit. "You were Robbie's friend, Mr. Saxon. He respected you, looked up to you. I want you to find out who killed him."

"Mr. Brody—"

"Kevin. Please."

"Kevin, private detectives don't investigate murders. Only on television. That's up to the police."

"Oh, fuck the police, they're no damn help at all! As soon as they found out Robbie had a record—"

"He did?"

Kevin Brody dropped his eyes. His lashes were long and dark blond and almost brushed his cheeks. He nodded. "Two prostitution arrests, one conviction. One arrest for lewd and lascivious behavior, suspended sentence." He raised his eyes to look at me, and there was defiance in them. "Sure, he was a hustler sometimes. He had to eat, too, you know, and acting jobs were few and far between. The name of the game is to *survive*."

"I'm not making any moral judgments," I said gently. "But you must know that in the eyes of the law everyone is the same when it comes to a capital crime. I'm sure the police are doing everything they can to—"

"The only reason they're bothering at all is that some bigwig got hurt at the same time."

"Bigwig?"

"That network guy. Steve Brandon."

I sat up a little straighter. Steven Brandon was the programming chief at Triangle Broadcasting Company and was generally regarded in Hollywood as this year's resident boy genius.

"How did Robbie know Steve Brandon?"

"He didn't."

I desperately wanted a cigarette, but it had been thirty-seven days and seventeen hours and I'm not sure how many minutes, and I wanted to be able to look myself in the eye the next morning when I shaved, so I simply chewed on the end of my ballpoint pen. "Maybe if you started at the beginning," I said, and pulled my yellow legal pad closer to me and wrote ROBBIE BINGHAM on the top line and underlined it three times.

Kevin uncrossed his legs and then crossed them again, this time with the left leg on top. It looked uncomfortable but he didn't seem to notice. "The last work Robbie did in pictures was *The Calico Cat,* Mr. Saxon, and you know how long ago that was. The whole industry has freaked out about AIDS. It's been a lean year for faggots."

I winced. I'd never liked that word, and the fact that a gay man was using it didn't make it much more palatable.

"So he was on the stroll on Santa Monica Boulevard a lot of the time. I helped him out as much as I could, but I don't make very much money. I'm a draftsman in the art department at Delacort's."

Delacort's was a mid-size department store just off Rodeo Drive in Beverly Hills, and since their men's briefs were priced at what was to most people a week's salary, I rarely shopped there.

I suppose I looked curious because Kevin's voice took on a defensive tone and he said, "Yes, we lived together. I'm the grieving widow."

"Kevin, I told you i don't make any moral judgments. I'm sorry about Robbie and I'll do what I can to help, but you have to stop thinking of me as the enemy just because I like girls."

He put his middle finger to his right eye and rubbed at the corner. "I'm sorry. This has been hell for me."

"Okay. Go on."

"Two and a half weeks ago—on the twelfth, it was—Robbie came home and said he'd tricked with a guy in a fancy BMW sedan. He'd gotten fifty dollars just to drive around with the guy for a few minutes—he didn't want to . . . you know, *do* anything. And Robbie said the guy made an appointment to meet him at nine o'clock the next morning and said he'd give him another hundred dollars just for running an errand. That was pretty early in the morning for tricking. But Robbie said it would probably be an easy hundred. Most tricks are only worth twenty-five or thirty."

"He didn't get a name or a phone number or a license plate or anything?"

"If you picked up a trick on Santa Monica, would you give out your name and number?"

I chewed the end of the pen some more. All I'd written on the yellow pad under Robbie's name was *12th* and *BMW*.

"That's all I know. The next morning they called me at the store to tell me he was dead."

"How did he die, Kevin?"

"He was driving a car down Cicada Drive in Bel Air and it exploded. The police said it was a bomb."

I wrote *bomb—ck. bomb squad* on the pad. Then I wrote over *bomb* three times until it stood out darkly among the other notes.

"Kevin, was there anyone—I'm sorry, but I have to ask this—who might have wanted to hurt Robbie? A jilted lover?"

"No," he said emphatically. "We've been together for four years, Mr. Saxon. We were committed and monogamous." He gave a little moue. "The tricks didn't count. That was business."

"These—tricks. Perhaps one of them . . . ?"

He shook his head again. "Whores never give their right name. Don't you know that?"

"No, I guess I never thought about it. What about the car?"

"A rented Ford Escort. Paid for with a stolen credit card."

"It couldn't have been Robbie who rented it?"

"Robbie would never steal a credit card. Or anything else. My God, once he found a wallet with a hundred thirty-eight dollars inside and he insisted on calling the owner up and returning it. And he was broke on his ass at the time, too." His eyes narrowed. "The cheap motherfucker didn't even offer a reward."

I underlined *Ford Escort* on my pad. "What did Steven Brandon have to do with this? Where did he fit?"

"He happened to be driving alongside Robbie when—when it happened. He's in the hospital, but he's going to live."

"What was the name of the car rental place, Kevin?"

"How in hell should I know?" Kevin said in anguish.

Scribble, scribble, I went. "Where did Robbie—uh, I mean, was there a particular place or corner? Where he, uh, where he worked?"

"Santa Monica and Garden, usually. But sometimes, when the law is out and are looking to bust heads, the boys have to keep moving so they don't get hassled for loitering."

I turned a page on my yellow legal pad and pushed it toward Kevin. "I want you to write down the names of all your friends; yours and Robbie's," I said. "Addresses and phone numbers, too, if you know them, and places where they work, so I can reach them. And places where he, you know, hung out: bars or cafés or anyplace like that. Anything else you can think of that might help me. Write it all down."

Kevin took the pad and got a pencil out of the ceramic mug that I'd used to drink coffee from until it developed a hairline crack. After he'd written two names he looked up, and the pain on his face made me hurt, too.

"I don't have a lot of money," he said. "I can give you a hundred dollars now, and then later . . . Well, I'll get the money somehow."

Standing on the corner of Santa Monica and Garden, I thought grimly. "Don't worry about that," I said. "If you can just pick up my expenses, we'll see what happens. I might not be able to find out anything. And you should know, Kevin, that if I'm caught interfering in an ongoing police investigation it could mean my license. So I'm going to have to tiptoe around the edges of this thing for a while."

"I dig," he said. "That's cool." He thought for a few seconds. "The only place Robbie really hung out was a Mexican taco place near La Brea. I don't even know what the name of it was. Everyone just calls it La Casa Cucaracha."

I had the feeling that wasn't the restaurant's real name at all. It translated to "The Cockroach House."

"You never went to bars?"

"Lots of them. The only place we ever went on a regular basis was called The Trade Winds. As in 'rough trade.' Get it?"

"Got it. Any idea what Robbie was doing on Cicada Drive in Beverly Hills?"

"I haven't the slightest. I suppose it had something to do with the errand. For the well-dressed rich dude in the BMW."

"How do you know he was rich?"

"Robbie said. Expensive suit—"

"Wearing a suit?"

"What's that got to do with the price of tomatoes?"

"Maybe nothing, Kevin. I'm just trying to get the whole picture here. Did Robbie say anything else?"

"No, not that I can think of."

"Think harder."

"I am! Christ Almighty, don't you think I've been over this in my head about a million times?"

"About the car. Did Robbie say what color it was? What year? Two-door or four-door? Model?"

"He said new. Of course, it could be a few years old and just kept shiny and new-looking. He just said new BMW, and he said the guy was wearing an expensive gray suit."

"Anything else about the man? Looks; age; tall or short?"

Kevin's carefully tweezed brows knitted in concentration and he replayed in his mind a memory tape that must have been very painful for him. It took him almost a minute.

"No," he said, and then he quickly amended, "just one thing. He kept reiterating that the guy didn't want to—have sex with him. Robbie said he thought he was straight."

2

Jo Zeidler was my part-time office assistant. I call her that instead of my secretary because she doesn't do any of the things a secretary does, like take dictation or type or keep track of my important appointments. And she sure doesn't do any of those things secretaries used to do before they got liberated, like doing my Christmas shopping or making coffee. Jo is Jewish and doesn't believe in Christmas, and she's an almost compulsive drinker of Russian Caravan tea and probably couldn't make a cup of coffee if she had to. Jo's function was mainly to make sure my business didn't slip quietly under the waves because I forgot to send out bills or didn't return phone calls or because I was too lazy to do some important research myself. It was just this kind of research that she was holding in her hand now, standing in front of my desk and waving a manila file folder at me.

"Here you go," she said, "the life and times of Robbie Bingham."

"Thanks, Jo, you're aces," I said. I don't usually talk like that, like a character out of a Fitzgerald novel. Only to Jo, because we really love each other. Not in a boy-girl way. Jo is married to a waiter who writes abstruse screenplays, and for reasons which escape me she is very much in love with him. We loved each other in a friend-friend way, which is in the long run a lot better than the boy-girl way, because it tends to last. That didn't stop me from casting an admiring glance at Jo's tush as she turned to walk out of my office. But when you have someone who's smart and efficient and is looking out for your interests, who cares about you and fusses over you and worries why you're not married and settled down, who makes you chicken soup when you've got a cold (yes, Jo does that, she really does, Honest-to-God chicken soup), then tushes aren't very important.

She turned in the doorway, her gamin face shining as though freshly scrubbed, and she said, "Are you going into this one full time?"

"I don't know. If I have to."

"You're not getting paid."

"Money isn't everything."

"But it's an awful lot."

"Robbie was my friend, Jo."

"He was a guy you met on a movie and worked with for two weeks. You didn't have lunch together, you didn't hang around together—you *sure* didn't go out and pick up girls together."

"It's the same principle, no matter what."

Jo shook her head, and her dark close-cropped curls danced. "I hope you take this good care of me if I get murdered." She turned and went back into the outer office, and I shuddered. There were some things people just didn't joke about; murder was one of them. I'd seen a few in my time. Not funny.

I poured myself a cup of coffee. My own coffee. I'd made it myself the way I did every morning, from freshly ground beans that I kept in the freezer at home and brought with me to the office. I'm pretty finicky about what I eat and drink, and since coffee is one of my passions I always drink the best, even when I can't afford it, which is most of the time.

I sat back down behind my desk and opened the folder: Robert Everett Bingham. Born January 11, 1962, in Wichita Falls, Texas. Died June 13, 1986, in Beverly Hills, California. Twenty-four years old. Getting a little long in the tooth to be selling his ass on Santa Monica Boulevard. Jo had gotten hold of a copy of Robbie's "composite," an eight-by-ten collage of four photographs of him in various outfits and poses, used by all actors to show how versatile they can be and how many different "looks" they had. Poor Robbie. His looks were all the same. He was quite handsome, well muscled (three of the four photographs showed a lot of skin), and yet around the mouth and eyes was a softness, a femininity that the camera couldn't hide. There must have been a million Robbie Binghams around Hollywood, kids who have been told all their lives how handsome they were and that they ought to be in movies, and they show up on the buses and trains and planes and wait for someone who has the power to do something about it to realize what their parents and friends had been telling them for years and put them in a movie and make them a star. When it didn't happen, some of them went back home to Texas or Iowa, defeated and broken, and took up careers and family life and all the good old middle-class American values, and some special spark went out of them forever. The taste of defeat stays on the tongue and on the soul for a long time. The luckier ones got jobs waiting tables or selling sportswear at the May Company and began thinking of themselves as Southern Californians and found a new life and assimilated. The stubborn ones, the ones who could never take no for an answer, often had to sell their bodies on the street. A few, like Robbie Bingham, even wound up dead.

I tried to imagine what it must have been like for a young man growing up to come to the realization that he was sexually attracted to other men, something that is not even blinked at in New York or Chicago or Miami or Los Angeles or San Francisco but must cause seismic waves in a place like Wichita Falls, Texas. Small wonder Robbie had gotten out and come west.

I briefly scanned the notes Kevin Brody had put on my yellow pad, then turned to the notes Jo had made from a conversation with the Beverly Hills Police Department. Robbie Bingham had been traveling north on Cicada Drive at

9:02 A.M. on the morning of June 13 when an explosive device under the hood of his car had detonated, killing him and injuring the driver of a car next to his, who happened to be Steven Brandon of Triangle Broadcasting Company. Not very much on which to hang your hat. I hesitated a moment, then dialed the number of the LAPD and asked to speak with Lieutenant Joe DiMattia.

"Listen, Saxon," came the high gravelly voice when I had identified myself, "I'm having the kind of morning I wouldn't wish on—you. I don't need your shit, okay?"

Joe didn't like me, because I had dated his wife before he'd met her and every time he looked at me or heard my voice his overactive imagination ate out his liver like Prometheus's vulture.

"Joe, I need a favor."

"I wouldn't give you the sweat off my ass, you know that."

"Would I ask you if it wasn't important? A friend of mine got offed, and I need the details."

"Since when do you have friends?"

"I've only got a few, and if people are going to go around murdering them I won't have any at all."

I heard him exhale. I could almost smell the garlic over the phone. "Name?"

"Bingham. Robert Bingham. He got killed on the thirteenth on Cicada Drive."

DiMattia sounded exasperated. "That's in Beverly Hills, anus," he said. "I don't have those files here."

"Your phone doesn't dial out? I have their number."

He paused for a moment. He really couldn't stand me, and I never knew why he always helped me when I asked his assistance. He was a Sicilian, about five eight and wide as a rhinocerous. The years and his mother's red clam sauce had taken a step or two off Joe's best time, but he was still pretty formidable, especially since he wore a gun and badge. I liked to think he always cooperated with me because he respected my abilities. I had helped him break a couple of cases some years back, and maybe he figured that despite his dislike for me, he owed me.

"I'll call when I get time," he said, and hung up without any parting pleasantries. That was DiMattia.

I got up and put on my jacket.

"Where are you off to?" Jo asked as I came into the outer office.

I almost answered, and then my common sense took over. "You wouldn't believe me if I told you."

Santa Monica Boulevard runs from the Silverlake area of Los Angeles, where it intersects Sunset, clear out to the Pacific Ocean, and is one of the city's main arteries. I resist the temptation to pun and say main *drag* because from about Western Avenue on the east to Doheny Drive on the west, the boulevard is given over largely to homosexuals, and the surrounding area from Hollywood to West Hollywood is known locally as Boys Town. The western portion boasts many elegant men's shops featuring the more far-out punk-funk fashions, several trendy gay discos, and a few of the city's better dining establishments. The section of the street that runs through the heart of Hollywood is a combat zone for male prostitutes. I drove eastward, and on almost every corner there was a young, almost defiant-looking male who would peer intensely at each driver and give a slight nod of the head to indicate he was available. The modus operandi seemed to differ from that of the female hookers on Sunset and Hollywood Boulevards, who stood in groups of twos and threes; the boys were almost always alone.

At the corner of Garden Avenue and Santa Monica there was a traffic signal, and when it flashed red I stopped and looked at the young man standing on the corner who was looking at me. The rag top on my Fiat was down, and he strolled over to the curb.

"What's happening?" he said.

"Not too much," I said. "How about you?"

He shrugged. "Just trying to raise some money for a bus ticket back to Atlanta." I didn't believe him. There was no trace of Georgia in his speech. I didn't say anything and he said, "Probably twenty-five dollars would do it."

"Get in," I said.

He opened the passenger door and slid in easily. He was wearing a pair of light blue shorts that were very tight, and a shimmel shirt that showed off his flat, hard stomach. He hadn't shaved in a few days and his fuzzy beard and mustache were blond. He reached out his hand to shake mine. "My name's Brian," he said.

I shook his hand.

He said, "I don't have a place to go around here. I generally work in cars, so you'll have to put the top up on this thing."

"I just want to talk to you," I said.

"Are you a cop?"

I gave him my business card. He looked at it and then put it in his pocket and shrugged. "Conversation or head—still costs twenty-five dollars."

"You want to just drive around or go have a cup of coffee or something?"

"Coffee keeps me awake," he said, "and it's bad for the skin. I could use a beer, though."

"La Casa Cucaracha?"

He gave me a look. "You do this a lot?"

"First time."

The inside of the little Mexican restaurant was a lot cooler than the street outside. Other than its nickname and its menu it didn't seem to be very Mexican at all, but a lot like a lot of other hot dog and hamburger stands in Hollywood. I had to get the beers at the counter, a Coors for Brian and a Dos Equis for me. I took them back to the booth near the window where he sat, keeping an eye on the street outside.

"Thanks," he said as I handed him the beer. He drained half of it in one swallow. "I hate to be crass but I'm going to have to ask you for the twenty-five dollars up front."

I dug into my pocket for my wallet and gave him a ten and three fives. "I'm a friend of Robbie Bingham's."

He didn't flicker an eyelash. "So?"

"Did you know him?"

"I know a lot of people."

"That doesn't make you special. I want to know if you knew Robbie."

He shrugged.

"I've already paid my twenty-five bucks," I said.

"I'd rather give you head than talk."

"I'm afraid that's not an option."

He took another pull on the beer, not quite as deep this time. "Yeah. Okay, I knew him. Now what?"

"I wasn't kidding when I said I was a friend of his."

"Yeah?" He leaned forward suddenly, challenging. "Then who was his lover? His roommate?"

"Kevin Brody," I said.

He sat back, apparently satisfied but not quite ready to drop the smartass pose. "Go to the head of the class," he said.

"Look, Brian, I'm trying to find out what happened to him. I was wondering maybe if you could help me."

"He went *boom!* That's what happened to him."

"Come on!"

"You mean, do I know who killed him? Of course not, man! Whattaya think?"

"You, uh, work on the same corner. I thought you might have seen something, or someone."

"I'm too busy being careful of my own ass. That's how you

make it through the day on the street, Mr. Saxon: you mind your own business. I might make the same suggestion to you."

"Thanks, but that's not helping me."

"I can't help you. I saw Robbie talk to a lot of guys in cars that last day he was out. I didn't notice any of them any more than anyone else. Just a bunch of mostly middle-aged guys who are straight—or straight-looking—mostly married, who just want a new kick or are just curious as to what a dick tastes like. They all tend to be the same, except the rough trade."

"What about them?"

"They like the slim young boys, the punks, and they like to slap them around or to dominate them or make slaves out of them. Like that," he said. "You got a cigarette on you?"

"I quit."

"I quit once a month. It won't last."

"Thanks for the encouragement."

"It's part of our twenty-five-dollar special. Look, I don't know anything about what happened to Robbie. I'm too busy trying to make my own living, you know what I'm saying to you?"

Being reasonably conversant in English, I knew what he was saying to me.

"This rough trade business. Was Robbie into that?"

"No. Like I said, those guys look for slim young boys. Robbie was too buff."

"Buff?"

Brian flexed his muscle for me by way of explanation. "They much prefer guys who look like me."

"Are you into that?"

Brian met my gaze and held it. "It'll cost you more than twenty-five if you want to get rough."

I sipped my beer. "Can you tell me the names of any of the

guys on the boulevard here that Robbie was particularly close to? Anyone he hung out with?"

"It'll take me a few minutes to think. Long enough for you to go get me another beer."

I got up and went to the counter, annoyed with myself. Brian had a way about him, there was no getting around it. And although he didn't look or act feminine in any way, there was some indefinable arrogance in his manner that allowed him to say and do things a woman could get away with that a straight man never could. I brought back his second beer before he finished the first, and he remedied that quickly by draining the bottle as I approached.

"None of us hang around with each other when we aren't working," Brian said as I sat down, "so I'm not sure I can tell you who any of Robbie's friends were. But he seemed to be in here a lot with a spade dude name of Marvel." He accented the second syllable. "Marvel's a chicken," he went on, and when he noted my frown he explained, "a very young kid, maybe fifteen or sixteen. And Robbie kind of looked out for him when they were both working. Nothing was going on there, though. Robbie was really awfully hung up on Kevin that way. But he looked out for Marvel anyhow. I guess he felt kind of sorry for the kid. He's a little simple."

"He's retarded?"

"I'm no doctor," Brian said, "but he's goddamn slow, and he talks like he's got a mouthful of shit. I can't understand him, but I guess Robbie did."

"What's Marvel's last name?"

He looked at me as if I was the simple one and didn't deign to answer.

"Okay, where can I find him?"

"Don't ask me. Cruise the street," he said, "and look for a kid about fifteen, small for his age, kind of coffee-with-cream color. He usually wears blue jeans and a Rams T-shirt."

"Anybody else you can think of?"

"We all know each other, man," he said. "You could spend the next ten years talking to all the whores on this street, and they'd all say what I said: 'Yes, I knew Robbie. No, I didn't see anything that day. Why don't you talk to Marvel?'" He took another sip and wiped his mouth with the back of his hand, a gesture I've always associated more with truck drivers than with willowy male prostitutes. "I frankly think you're beating a dead horse," he said, and then laughed. "Or should I say, a dead whore?"

"You know, Brian, you're way too bright to be doing this."

"I'm too bright not to, Saxon."

"How do you mean?"

"Look," he said, "I'm twenty years old; I'm skinny and have a big dick. I've got about two more good years doing this, and I mean good years, because I pull down a couple hundred every day except during heavy rains and on Christmas. The way I figure it, in another two years I can go back to school, study economics, and get into something like the brokerage business. Don't laugh."

"I'm not laughing," I said. "But while you're pulling down your two hundred a day, aren't you worried about something like what happened to Robbie? Aren't you scared of herpes or syphilis or AIDS?"

"No. Why should I be scared? I could give it all up and go get a job in a shoe store and get hit by a truck. Life's full of little risks. That's what makes it fun. Isn't that why you're in the detective business? And isn't that part of the excitement of being an actor?"

I was so startled I jumped. He snickered. "Robbie was so jazzed about being in that damn movie he made us all watch it on TV over at The Trade Winds. I recognized you right away when I walked up to your car. I also figured why you were here. It wasn't to trick."

"How could you be sure?"

"Johns don't drive around with their convertible tops down in broad daylight. Or at night, either, far as that goes."

"You're all right, Brian. I wish you luck."

"We make our own luck, Saxon. That was the problem with Robbie."

"How so?"

"I told you, people survive out here by being careful and watching their own ass. Well, if you knew Robbie you knew the way he was. Open, trusting, kind of naive. If anyone I knew on the boulevard was going to get hurt, it was probably going to be Robbie."

I stood up and gave him a handshake. "You've been a help, Brian, whether you know it or not."

"Sure," he said. "And if you ever want to get into a scene— I know you're straight, but if you'd get a kick out of watching me get it on with your old lady, say, let me know. I go both ways."

Marvel wasn't too hard to find. Brian had given me an excellent description, and I hadn't gone four blocks down the boulevard before I spotted him on the corner, leaning against a No Parking sign. As promised, he was wearing a gray Los Angeles Rams T-shirt with the team's logo on an iron-on decal across his slim chest. His hands were hooked into the empty belt loops of his Levi's. Both shirt and pants were very faded with hard wear, but they looked clean. I slowed down my car, and his brown eyes flashed invitation at me, but I was not about to spend any more money on male prostitutes.

"Marvel?" I said.

He looked surprised, and then frightened. He jumped back a step or two, ready to run, and I held out my hand and said, "It's all right, Marvel. I'm a friend of Robbie's."

His straight black brows wrinkled into a frown. "Robbie?" he repeated.

"Robbie Bingham. Your friend."

"He dead."

"I know, Marvel," I said. "That's why I'm here. Come on, let me buy you some lunch."

His child's face looked suspicious. "You want a date?" he said. "You ain't a cop?"

I leaned over and opened the passenger door. "Come on, Marvel, I'm not going to hurt you."

He put his hand on the door but didn't get in, not right away. He leaned in to me and he said, "You a friend of Robbie's for sure?"

"For sure, for sure," I said in the manner of San Fernando Valley teenagers. "Come on, I want to help."

He got in the car slowly. He looked younger than sixteen, more like thirteen. There was the barest suggestion of fuzz on his upper lip, and his light brown arms were hairless. He sat there staring straight ahead, obviously frightened, and didn't close the door, as if at any moment he would fly off down the block. Then he looked at me, and his eyes got wet and he said once more, "Robbie dead." And then he started to cry.

So there I was, in the middle of Santa Monica Boulevard in an open convertible with an underage male hooker crying his heart out in my passenger seat. I wanted to comfort him but finally settled for saying, "Come on, Marvel. It's okay." That was pretty lame.

I took him to a nearby coffee shop. Showing up with two street hustlers inside an hour at the Cucaracha was bound to attract more attention than I cared to enjoy. He asked for a big hamburger, finished it and a milk shake, and then repeated the order. I had coffee, which tasted lousy on top of the beer. When Marvel asked if he could have an ice cream sundae for dessert I began to think it would have been cheaper to pay him the twenty-five dollars.

"Robbie, he the only one decent to me," Marvel said

wistfully when he had finished his lunch. "Shit, why he have to die like that?"

I said gently, "I'm trying to find out, Marvel, and that is why I wanted to talk to you. I know he was your friend and I know you want to help."

Marvel was trying very hard not to cry. He nodded in agreement. Then he said, "But I don't know nothing. Everybody say I jus' dumb. Jus' *dumb!*"

"Did you ever go to school, Marvel?"

He nodded. "Long time ago. Long time."

"Well, I don't think you're dumb," I said. "And I'll bet you can help me, and help your friend, too."

"Nobody help him," Marvel said. "He dead."

Not dumb at all, I thought, even though he made me feel that way. "I'll bet that you and Robbie talked a lot, huh? I'll bet that he told you lots of things."

"He tol' me how to watch out for heat."

"Did he ever tell you about things that happened to him? People that he met?"

"Sometimes." Warily.

"Now, Marvel, on that last day, the last time you saw him—now, don't cry, it's okay—on that day, did he tell you about meeting a man who gave him fifty dollars, who was going to give him a lot more money, a hundred dollars, the next day? Did he say anything about that, Marvel?"

The boy was concentrating really hard for a few seconds, and then he broke into a relaxed grin as if he'd just gotten rid of a sharp gas pain. "Yeah," he breathed, drawing out the word.

I leaned forward, excited. "Can you remember what he told you? Anything?"

"He say he meet this cat with big bucks, jus' want to talk. Like you."

I didn't like the comparison but couldn't do too much

about it. "He say," the boy went on, "he gonna give Robbie a hunderd nex' day."

"Is that all he said?"

"He say that cat gonna he'p him get into movies."

I finished the dregs of my coffee, stale and cold as it was. "Where do you live, Marvel?"

He waved his hand vaguely. "Hollywood."

"What street? Who do you live with?"

His eyes got very large and he looked around nervously. I realized I'd frightened him. He was, after all, just a little boy.

"That's all right, Marvel," I said.

I paid the check and together we walked out into the parking lot. I wanted to do something for him, maybe give him some money, but somehow I felt funny about it in a way I had not with Brian. I said, "Can I drive you somewhere?"

"It be okay," he said. "I walk." He started off across the parking lot toward the sidewalk.

"Wait," I called after him, "what if I want to talk to you again?"

He didn't answer and he didn't turn around, just kept walking, his eyes on the pavement in front of his feet. I watched him until he disappeared around the corner of the building out of sight. I realized I was abandoning a child on the streets, but I told myself that I had no responsibility for him. He was not my child. Or he was. They were all our children.

3

I called Jo from a pay phone. She'd managed to get the name of the car rental agency from DiMattia, and I wrote it in my notebook. It was in Burbank, the San Fernando Valley. It was my least favorite part of Los Angeles; the absolute Smog Capital of the World. I said to Jo, "Any other calls?"

"Marsh called." Marsh Zeidler was her husband.

"For me?"

"No, silly, for me. Why would he call you? I swear, you're spending too much time with those gays."

"Why did you mention it, then?"

"You asked if someone else had called; I told you. You never specified the calls had to be for you." Jo's hobby was putting me on.

"Keep it up," I said heavily, "and dearly as I love thee, we cross swords."

"Just promise not to hit me with your purse," she said.

I drove over the Cahuenga Pass to Burbank, where the Mayan Auto Rental office was located, and confronted the attendant, a young girl wearing the bright yellow uniform of the company, which included the kind of military cap known in the army as a "piss cutter." Women in uniforms either look unbearably pert and adorable or they resemble grain sacks. This particular lady was not pert and adorable.

"Hi," she said, "can I help you?"

I gave her my business card and showed her the copy of my PI license. "I'm conducting an investigation for Intertel Insurance," I said. I know it's a lousy name, but I made it up on the spur of the moment. "About that car of yours that was bombed a few weeks ago—"

She made a noise that I supposed expressed distaste. It came out something like *"Eeeeeue!"*

"I understand that the credit card used to obtain the vehicle was stolen?"

"It wasn't me," she said. "It happened on Jennifer's shift."

"That's all right," I said. "Do you suppose you could let me have a little peek at the paperwork?"

"The cops—I mean, the police—took the originals. We had to make Xerox copies."

"A Xerox copy will do nicely, thanks."

She squatted down in front of a file cabinet behind the counter, her short skirt riding up to show me a lot more of her chubby thigh than I cared to see, and went through several manila folders before she found the document she sought.

"Here it is," she said. "I can't let you take it out of the office."

"No need, if you'll give me a few minutes to look at it. I promise I won't steal it."

"I didn't think you were going to *steal* it. Guy!"

I said with great dignity, "I shall try to be worthy of your trust."

"Guy! You talk funny!" *Guy* seemed to be an interjection used by those who did not wish to blaspheme by saying "God!" but realized however dimly that *gosh* and *gee* had gone the way of the passenger pigeon and the great auk.

I took out my notebook and jotted down the pertinent data. The car had been rented at 7:24 P.M. on the evening of June 12, the night before Robbie Bingham died. The Visa card was in the name of a Raymond Sheed, and the address given was on Reese Place in Burbank, a nice middle-class residential neighborhood. The signature was a bold one, strong and definite, with a high capital *R* made with a vertical slash for the left side of the letter, after which the pen, obviously a ballpoint so it would register on the carbon copy, was removed before completing the round loop and then the diagonal. The *S* in Sheed was also large and had been printed instead of done in cursive style.

I dutifully noted the mileage on the car when it had been checked out, and the price: $22.95 per day, plus eleven cents a mile after the first hundred. The man who had masqueraded as Sheed had said he would need the car for about four days. That had evidently been another lie.

"If I need to talk to this Jennifer," I said, handing the form back to the girl, "where can I find her?"

"She comes on at six," the girl said. "Except she's usually late, which really gets me p.o.'d, because I'd like to get home too, you know."

"I know," I said.

I drove over to The Coach Room to review my notes and have my first drink of the day. The Coach Room was just about the only place I went over in Burbank because they carried my favorite Scotch, Laphroaig. And since Burbank was home to several movie and TV studios I was not unknown to Sean, the barman.

"I haven't seen you since the war," Sean said by way of salutation.

"Which war is that?"

"The big one," he said, as if that explained it. "You must not be working these days or you'd be out here."

"There are other studios in town," I said as he placed a double, neat, and a water back in front of me. "However, you just happen to be right, curse your Irish soul."

"If you'd drink decent Irish whiskey instead of that smoky crap you guzzle, you'd have a sharper mind, a clearer complexion, more friends, and probably be a major star instead of a day player."

"It's not worth it to me," I told him, and took a sip. The

Scotch was indeed smoky, a single malt whisky unlike any other. And I've tasted a considerable amount of Scotch in my day. For me, Irish whiskey can't compare.

"What brings you out here, Saxon? Show biz or your other gig?"

"They always seem to intertwine," I said. "How's it going?"

"Don't ask," he said. "Between raising the price of a pop because of the new booze tax and them cutting out happy hour and cracking down on the DUIs on the streets, people have quit going out to drink. And because of herpes and AIDS and God knows what other loathsome sexually transmitted foulness going around, people just don't cruise bars to get laid anymore. They go home to their wives instead. It's depressing."

"Next time I won't ask," I said.

We batted it around for a few more minutes and then the bar started filling up with the five o'clock office escapees and Sean got very busy, which gave the lie to what he'd just told me, and that gave me some time to think. On a hunch, I got up and went out into the foyer and looked up Raymond Sheed in the Burbank phone book, and I found him.

The voice that answered the phone sounded as though it belonged to a very nice lady; she told me that her husband was not at home. Further inquiry on my part revealed that he was working late this evening over at the Triangle Broadcasting studios in Burbank, hard by NBC, Warner Brothers (I know it's called The Burbank Studios now, but for years it was home to the likes of Bogart and Cagney and Bette Davis and even Ronald Reagan, and for me it would always and forever be Warner Brothers), and the Walt Disney studios.

I called my friend Jay Dean in the casting department at Triangle, guessing that, like most middle-management TV folk, he was working late. I guessed right, and I asked him if he could leave my name at the gate so I could get on the lot that evening.

"Sure, no problem," he said. "What's up?"

"I'm going to sit in the audience at 'Deal of a Lifetime.' Maybe I can win myself a new microwave."

"You're a strange person, you know that? Come on over; I'll call down right now. Try not to get into any trouble on the set, will you? You have a tendency to get people mad enough to hit you, and then you hit them back and the roof falls in."

"I'll keep my hands in my pockets," I promised.

"It's your mouth I worry about," Jay said.

I went back to the bar, finished my drink, paid my tab, and said good-bye to Sean. He was a throwback to what bartenders were supposed to be, to what they were before the job was filled by would-be actors, moonlighting stockbrokers, and girls with tight T-shirts who were putting their boyfriends through trade school.

The Triangle studios and executive offices were not two minutes' drive from The Coach House—except at five-thirty in the afternoon, which happened to be when I was making the trip. So some twenty minutes later I rolled through the gates after a rigorous questioning from the potbellied security guard. I parked in the VIP lot and headed for Studio 7, where America's top-rated game show, "Deal of a Lifetime," was to tape five episodes that evening.

When I arrived the festivities had not yet begun; the audience had not yet been ushered in but was still standing in a long queue on the sidewalk outside, and the crew was making last-minute checks on the sets and props so that when the host, the genial Scott Raney, came out wearing his pasted-on smile and his wardrobe from Giorgio's in Beverly Hills and asked the audience if they were ready to make the deal of a lifetime, everything he reached for would be right where it was supposed to be. At least that was what some of the crew was doing. The rest of them were standing around drinking coffee and eating the doughnuts the "Deal" production company had thoughtfully supplied. Why anyone would want to eat a glazed doughnut at six o'clock in the evening was a question I couldn't answer, but there they were. People who work in television will eat anything as long as they don't have to pay for it.

I asked one of the few men actually working where I could find Raymond Sheed. He stopped, looked around the studio, and pointed to one of the guys sitting on chairs, and I walked over and introduced myself.

Raymond Sheed was a large, paunchy, balding man whose scant few strands of hair were sandy-reddish and not very artfully combed to cover his shiny skull. He wore glasses and his skin was an acne survivor. He looked up in a noncurious way when he found out who I was.

"I told the police everything," he said. "My wallet had been missing for two days and I called up and canceled the credit cards. I guess I wasn't quick enough."

"Where did you lose your wallet, Mr. Sheed?"

"If I knew that it wouldn'ta been lost. But I think it disappeared somewhere on the lot here. Sometimes I leave it in my jacket in the prop locker. I don't ever worry about it because I never carry my money in there."

"Where do you carry your money?"

"Where do you think?" he said. He pulled out a cheap gold-plated money clip with a big dollar sign on it. It was stuffed with lots of bills. I couldn't tell their denominations but the one on top was a fifty; there was no mistaking old Ulysses Simpson Grant. Network-level television prop men did all right on the money side; they made more than ninety-five percent of the actors did, anyway.

"Did you tell the police your wallet had been stolen?"

"No."

"Why not?"

"What were they gonna do, put out an APB? Besides, I didn't think it was stolen; I thought it was lost. You know what? I still think so."

"Why?"

"Because a week later I got it back."

"How?"

He shrugged and lit a cigarette. It was an old-fashioned filterless Camel. It smelled wonderful. "A big manila envelope showed up in the prop shop one day with my name on it. I open it up, there's the wallet. Nothing missing, not my driver's license, nothing."

"And did you notify the police about that?"

He shook his head.

"Surely you know, Mr. Sheed, that your credit card was used to rent a car that was involved in a murder? Didn't you think the police might like to hear about that? It might have given them a lead."

He stood up. He was almost as tall as I and outweighed me by about fifty pounds.

"Look. I been with Triangle twenty-three years. I been in the union thirty-three. Two years from now I retire: I got a nice pension coming in from the network, I got good retirement benefits from the union, I take my wife and we go up north near Morro Bay and we live in the little cabin I bought sixteen years ago. So no trouble, no bullshit, no taking off work to go down to headquarters and look at pictures, no trouble with the brass, and I get to stay on this show, which is a piece of cake because it only tapes once a week or so and the fringe benefits are good, if you get my drift, because when Scott Raney-in-the-Face says, 'Tell 'em what they've won, Bill!' and Bill says, 'A brand new washer and dryer!' it's me that supplies the washer and dryer that they take the pretty pictures of with the broad standing there pointing at it, and when the need arises it's me that takes the washer and dryer or whatever home to the missus, or to my friendly neigh- borhood fence, and everybody knows it but they turn their heads because that's just one of the perks of propping a show like this. So I don't call no cops and with any luck they don't call me, and that includes private cops, so if you'll excuse me . . . ?"

"Just a minute more, please, Mr. Sheed."

"Look, why don't you go sit in the audience? Tonight they're giving away a trip to Hawaii."

"I'm allergic to poi and I hate Don Ho," I said. "On the day you first noticed your wallet was missing—"

"That was the eleventh."

"Two days before the murder."

"If you say so."

"Can you remember where you were that day?"

"In the morning I played nine holes of golf up at Candle Wood. I had my wallet with me then because I had to use my credit card for lunch after." He grinned. "I lost, I bought."

"And in the afternoon?"

"In the afternoon I was right here; we taped five shows that evening. I was getting into the car about midnight when I noticed the wallet wasn't in my jacket pocket. I came back into the studio and looked around for it, but this is a pretty big place and I figured it was a lost cause. The next day we tore everything down here so they could put up the set for the Dean Martin special."

"Now try to think, Mr. Sheed," I said.

"Look, I really got to go."

"Just one more—little—question. Did anything unusual happen that day here at the studio? Anything out of the ordi- nary? Anything at all?"

He put his fingers under his eyeglasses and rubbed the bridge of his nose. There was a deep red indentation on either side of his nose where many years of spectacle wearing had worn their grooves. "Well, there's always new people here for a game show like this. New contestants. But the security is so tight here since they caught 'em rigging game shows back in the fifties, they treat those poor bastards like it was Auschwitz. They don't even let 'em go to the john by themselves."

"Anything else?"

"I don't think so. Some of the big program brass came down to watch the early tapings, but they do that every few weeks anyway. I think they like it because everyone gets nervous and starts thinking about cancellation and then they work harder and make more money for good old Triangle."

"Was Steven Brandon one of the brass that was here?"

"Hell, no. He ain't brass, he's Golden Boy. He doesn't fart around with daytime game shows."

"There might have been fingerprints on the wallet."

"Couldn't tell it by me," he said. "I doubt if they're still there now, though. Look, Mr. . . . ?"

"Saxon."

"What's your interest in all this?"

I always wonder why people ask you your name and then don't use it. I said, "Intellectual curiosity. Thanks for your time, Mr. Sheed."

"Hell, don't mention it," he said, and kind of lumbered away. Like a coyote, I sniffed the air where the smoke from his Camel still lingered. Habits die hard, and I found myself profoundly annoyed with Sheed for having the bad manners to smoke in front of me.

I started out the studio door and just made it to the hallway when I ran into Scott Raney, the host of "Deal of a Lifetime." He gave me a searching look and then said, "Hi, Scott Raney," and tucked his salmon-colored five-by-seven cards under his left arm so he could shake hands. "I'm sorry, I don't remember your name, but I know I've seen you act on TV and in the movies. Hey, I am really flattered you dropped by to see the show. That makes me feel really good when my peers think enough of me and of the show to come by and cheer us on."

"I didn't—"

"Listen, tell Melody where you're going to be sitting. I'd kind of like to introduce you to the studio audience. They'd get a kick out of it, I know, seeing an actor like you. I can't do it on camera during the show; then we'd have to pay you and I think we're over budget already. But before the first show starts I'd love to have you stand up and take a bow. It'd make me really proud." He pumped my hand again. "Hey, thanks again for coming around. Appreciate it." He turned his head and called over his shoulder, "Melody!" without looking, and a young girl with a sallow complexion, stringy hair, a Boston Red Sox sweatshirt, and jeans that bagged over her practically invisible butt, came running up brandishing a clipboard and a felt pen.

"Make sure he gets a VIP seat down front; I want to introduce him to the studio audience. You recognize him, don't you? Hell of an actor. See you later." And he was gone.

He had absolutely no idea what my name was. He just vaguely recognized the face.

"Hi-I'm-Melody-the-PA," she said in a singsong. "I know you're an actor, I've seen you in something. What's your name?"

"Hoot Gibson."

She wrote it down. "Where are you going to be sitting?"

"Tall in the saddle," I said.

I got out of there fast. The temptation to stick around and hear Scott Raney ask a long-dead silent movie cowboy to stand up and take a bow was well-nigh overwhelming. But I had other things to do.

○ 4 ○

Jennifer was wearing the same silly paramilitary skirt and jacket in hot yellow as had her compatriot at Mayan Auto Rental, but there the resemblance ended. She had a gorgeous mane of light brown hair, very blue eyes, and a figure that can best be described as lush. In her high heels she was almost as tall as I am, and a good bit of that height was legs. Her tan bespoke many hours at the beach or in a tanning booth, and the only makeup she wore was a light lipstick and some eyeliner. I almost wished I needed to rent a car.

"It's been quite a while," she said, "so my memory is a little bit hazy. But it seems to me, and I told the police the same thing, that the gentleman was in his late forties or so, very nicely dressed, kind of thinning hair. Medium-tall."

"That doesn't sound hazy to me," I said, making notes.

"Well, the police came and talked to me a few days after the—accident. So I just told them everything I know. The name on his driver's license matched the one on his credit card, and that was Raymond Sheed."

"You didn't check the picture on the license?"

She smiled at me. "Can I see your driver's license?"

"Sure," I said, taking out my wallet. "Why?"

She looked at my license, then at me. "That doesn't look a whole lot like you, Mr. Saxon."

I looked at the picture and nodded. "You're right," I said, "it doesn't nearly do me justice."

Her laugh was merry. "Everybody looks odd on their CDL photo. Like passport pictures."

"I'll bet your passport picture is smashing."

"You'd lose your bet. Anyway, we usually just glance at the picture, and unless the person is a different sex or color than the photo we let it go."

"Was the man wearing glasses? Either in the picture or in person?"

"I don't remember the picture that well, but I'd say that he wasn't wearing glasses when he came in, no."

"You sure?"

"No, I'm not," she said, "but I don't think so."

"Do you wear glasses, Jennifer?"

"Contacts."

"Did you ever?"

Her eyes danced. "Did I ever what?"

"Wear glasses?"

"In high school. I was kind of an ugly duckling, tall and gawky."

"I think I like the swan better."

"Me, too."

"Now, when you were gawky and ugly and you wore glasses, did you ever have those little red marks on either side of your nose? You know, where the glasses press in?"

"Sure."

"Okay, now think back if you can, Jennifer; it might be important. Did the man who used Raymond Sheed's credit card that night have those red marks on his nose?"

"No," she said, "I think I would have noticed that."

Then it was indeed not Raymond Sheed who had rented the ill-fated Ford Escort. That narrowed it down considerably—to about two million other guys who were in their late forties and had thinning hair.

"Anything else you can tell me? Anything at all?"

"Gee, I don't know." At least she didn't say "Guy!"

"Any little thing, even though you might not think it's important? Like, did the man seem nervous or anxious?"

She thought about it. "Just the opposite, I'd say."

"How do you mean?"

"He seemed like a no-nonsense type, the kind of guy that was used to getting good, efficient service. And . . ."

"Yes?"

"I don't know how to say this. It sounds stupid."

"Take a chance. I won't hold it against you."

She looked down at her fingernails, polished to match her lipstick. "He didn't hit on me."

"I guess that doesn't happen very often."

"I told you it was going to sound stupid."

"No, it doesn't, really."

"It's not that every guy who walks in here makes a move. But there is a certain type—guys like this one, who obviously have a little money and a good self-image. If they don't ask me to have a drink with them, or dinner, or tell me they're from out of town and could use someone to show them around the city, at least they kind of flirt. It's harmless most of the time, but it's there."

"And the false Mr. Sheed didn't flirt?"

"He hardly looked at me."

"You think he might have been gay?"

"Maybe. It's so hard to tell gay from straight anymore."

I put away my wallet and closed my notebook and put it in my jacket pocket, signaling that I was finished with any official business. "Tell me something," I said. "When these men flirt and ask you for drinks or dinner, do you ever go?"

"Sometimes."

"Good," I said. "How about dinner, then?"

"I work most nights."

"Most, but not all?"

"Why don't you give me your card? Maybe I'll call you."

"I just happen to have tomorrow open," I said.

I collected her home telephone number and told her I'd wait for her phone call. I also found out her last name was London, and I wondered if she might be an aspiring actress. Real people are just not named Jennifer London. I have a hard and fast rule about going out with actresses. They are most often very into themselves; they have to be, to survive in such a competitive profession. They also tend to want to go to "in" movie industry restaurants and sit facing the door in case someone important might come in. Actresses make lousy dates, and I avoid them in social situations. Of course, I wasn't sure that Jennifer London was an actress, now, was I?

I drove back over the Cahuenga Pass into Hollywood and stopped off at my office to see if there were any messages. Kevin Brody had called at six. I called him back but there was no answer. I switched on my black-and-white TV that I keep in the office for Dodger games. There wasn't much on except syndicated reruns of ten-year-old sitcoms, a local magazine-type show that was paying a visit to an aerobics class for senior citizens, and a game show even more witless than "Deal of a Lifetime." Not exactly riveting TV fare, so I turned on the radio instead and pulled out a book I'd been reading a paragraph at a time and tried to kill a few hours. I couldn't keep my mind on it and decided it wasn't my fault; it just wasn't a very good book.

By the time the phone rang I'd done all the fantasizing about Jennifer that I needed to do and was so bored I was even glad to hear Joe DiMattia's gravelly voice on the other end of the line.

"Write this down, schmuck, because I'm not going to repeat it," he said. No hello, how are you, this is Joe, glad I caught you in the office. That was DiMattia. He had the manners of a warthog. "Your pal Robert Bingham was a dickie-licker, did you know that? I always figured that about you but I don't like to accuse anyone without some proof."

"Joe, if your best friend is black, does that mean you are?"

"Yeah, sure. Wait till I tell Marie."

Marie was his wife. "Anyway, the car was rented with a phony credit card."

"I know all that."

"Why the fuck didn't you say so and save me the trouble? You think I got nothing better to do than—"

"What else, Joe?"

"The bomb was a very simple device, four sticks of dynamite jerry-rigged to go off by remote control, the same kind of little black box you'd use to switch channels on your TV set without having to get up off your lazy ass. Which means that the guy with the controls had to be within about three hundred feet of the car when the bomb blew."

"Exactly where was the device on the Ford?"

"Tucked up over the right front wheel. The Bev Hills bomb guys said it was a pretty neat job."

"And exactly where was the car at the time of the explosion?"

"At the corner of Cicada and Roscoemare, heading south on Cicada."

"And the time?"

"Nine forty-five A.M."

"What about the man in the other car?"

I heard him rustle papers. "You must know about this, since it's show-bizzy," Joe said, and I heard him breathing through his nose. "Steven Brandon, vice president in charge of programming at Triangle Broadcasting. Brain concussion, lacerations of face and neck from flying glass, broken left shoulder and collarbone, and possible partial loss of hearing in left ear. His Mercedes was totaled."

"Joe, does Brandon live on or near Cicada Drive?"

A pause while he looked, then, "No, Malibu. I can't give you the address, though," he said.

"I don't want it. What hospital did they take him to after the blast?"

"Saint Iggy in Santa Monica. Listen, you schmuck, you dick around with this case where you're not sposed to, the BHPD is gonna put your nuts in a wringer. I had to tell them why I was asking."

I gritted my teeth. "You had to, huh?"

"Who's your client, anyway?"

"You know better than to ask, Joe."

"Why is it, Saxon, that I leave my ass waving out in the breeze for you and you can't even answer a simple question?"

"It's obvious, Joe: you said it, I'm a schmuck."

He called me a lot of other things before he hung up. At one time, because of Marie, I thought DiMattia really loathed me. But lately he had either mellowed or he was starting to really enjoy the abuse he vigorously heaped on me. Either way, I figured if I ever ran afoul of the law and he found out about it, it would be six months before anyone ever discovered where I was, and by that time it would be too late.

It was now well past nine o'clock and the only shows on TV were prime-time soap operas, so I didn't even bother with the television set. I locked up the office and headed for Santa Monica Boulevard again.

Boys Town was busier at night than it had been in mid-afternoon. The sidewalks were crowded with pedestrians, but there was not a woman in sight, and no men past the age of thirty. I had a feeling I wasn't going to have a very nice evening.

The Trade Winds had its own parking lot but there wasn't a single vacant space, so I had to park on one of the side streets and walk back. There was a large muscular young man in black leather standing by the doors checking to see that all who entered were of legal drinking age. He didn't even ask me for my ID. In spite of a full head of gray hair I look younger than my age, but I sure as hell don't look nineteen, either.

The blast of sound that hit me as I walked in the door had a physical impact, it was that loud. The music was almost unidentifiable, so thunderous was it, although as a jazz buff and a hard-rock hater I probably would not have recognized the tune anyway. The air was thick with smoke and the smells of sweat and after-shave, and it was so dark I could barely make out the fake palm trees that were the only decor. The lights were all of a pinkish hue, and there were damn few of them, too. I could dimly see the couples gyrating on the small dance floor, but I didn't need bright lights to know they were all male. I pushed my way through the crowd to the bar, winding up between a young man with a receding hairline who wore white sailcloth duck pants, a V-necked maroon sweater with no shirt, and Gucci loafers on his sockless feet, and a large, bushy man in an exercise suit whose beard and shaggy hair made him look like a pirate. There were two bartenders on duty, both in skintight lavender T-shirts with the club's logo on the front and skimpy white shorts. I ordered a Heineken and, with some difficulty due to the cramped quarters, turned around to watch what was going on. I guess my eyes were growing accustomed to the gloom because I was able to see faces out on the floor and at the small Formica tables shoved too close together. Almost everyone who was not dancing was smoking, making me painfully aware that it was now forty days exactly since my last cigarette. The insides of my nostrils were stinging. The beer tasted lousy.

"Hi," said the guy in the maroon sweater.

"Hi," I said.

"Would you like to dance?"

"Not right now."

"Well, get her!" he said, and walked away. His departure gave me a scintilla more room at the bar, and I was grateful for it. I had started feeling claustrophobic. I was creating all sorts of scenarios in my mind as to what I might say if someone I knew saw me sipping a beer at The Trade Winds.

I turned back to the bartender. "Has Kevin Brody been in tonight?"

"A few hours ago, but he left."

"Did he say where he was going?"

He looked at me suspiciously. "Who are you?"

"A friend of his."

"Uh-huh," he said, and moved away. I don't think he believed me.

Other than once in San Juan, when I had walked into one by mistake, this was my first experience in a gay bar. I think I was as uncomfortable as one might suppose, but no more so than if I had been dragged to a recital of German lieder. It just didn't happen to be my thing, that was all.

I took another long swallow and the shaggy man next to me said, "What do you want with Kevin?" His voice was surprising in that it was high and flutey, not what one would have expected from such a bearlike fellow.

"He left a message on my answering machine and I thought I might catch him here. You know him?"

The bear nodded gravely. "Kevin's hurting," he said in a mournful tone. "Real bad."

"I know."

"You're not going to hassle him, are you?"

"Not at all."

"He doesn't need hassles."

"Nobody does, do they?"

He looked at me. "You don't belong here, do you?"

I shrugged. "It's a public place."

"You know what I mean."

"Yeah, I guess I do. No, you're right."

"Are you heat?"

"No."

"Just looking for something strange, huh?"

"No. Just looking for Kevin."

"I don't want to see anyone get messed over."

"Neither do I."

"If you hassle Kevin I'm going to take it personally."

"I told you before."

"Sure," he said. "You told me." He turned his back on me. I had the feeling that he could tear off one of my legs with no trouble at all, and I silently resolved to make certain he didn't become so inclined. The Scotch I'd had earlier and the beer I was drinking were assaulting my kidneys, but no power on earth could force me into the men's room of The Trade Winds.

I was feeling a little silly, and frustrated as well. I didn't know why I was here, I didn't know what I had hoped to gain in the way of pertinent information, I was uncomfortable, and I was drinking an unwanted drink and inhaling other people's smoke while denying myself my own. I finished the beer and headed for the door, and when I got outside I gratefully gulped the fresh air.

I walked to the corner and turned down the street to where my car was parked. Before I could get in I was grabbed from behind by a powerful pair of arms, squeezed, lifted off my feet, then shaken and dropped again. Then I was spun around and slammed against the side of the car. While I was catching my breath I saw it was the large shaggy man with the high voice.

"Hey!" I said. Not very original, but it's hard to be creative when you've had the breath squeezed out of you.

"You better start talking, friend," he piped.

"I've got nothing to say."

He took my shoulders and pulled me toward him, then bounced me off the car again. "I think you do. Who are you, anyway?"

I started to reach for my wallet to give him a business card, and he rammed me into the car a third time. "God damn it, stop it!" I said.

He stepped back to hit me, which gave me the legroom I needed. I kicked him in the kneecap, very hard, and he screamed, lifting his injured leg, and that's when I hit him in the face. Off balance, he went down like a felled redwood and lay there for a second or two, stunned, and then he started to cry. He brought his injured knee up to his chest and cradled it with his hands and rocked and sobbed. I did nothing but stand there, feeling like a jerk, and waited for him to simmer down. It took about a minute.

"Come on," I said, reaching down with my hand to assist him, "get up."

"I can't. I think you broke my kneecap."

"No, I didn't," I said, not entirely sure. "Come on, get up on your feet and walk around a little so it doesn't stiffen up on you."

He took my hand and pulled himself upright, and I feared for my back. He was a big one, about two hundred eighty pounds, even though much of that was beard and hair. He flexed his hurt leg gingerly and then took my advice and started walking on it. He was limping, but nothing was broken.

"I'm sorry," I said finally. "I don't like being shoved around."

He waved his hand at me, dismissing my apology, and marched back and forth a few times, then leaned on the fender of my car. It was a little car, and it groaned under the weight. "My fault," he said, sniffling, and I wasn't going to argue with him. He rubbed his knee, and then rubbed his cheekbone where I'd hit him. If he'd had both feet on the ground I couldn't have toppled him.

Finally he said, "When you're as big as I am, you start thinking that getting rough is the only way to go."

"Most of the time it is," I said. "No hard feelings?"

He shook his head. "I just want to protect Kevin from getting hassled."

"You're a friend of his?"

He nodded. "Barry Haworth."

I shook his outstretched hand. He had a grip like a wolf trap.

"I'm a friend of Kevin's, too," I said. "And I was a friend of Robbie's."

"You knew Robbie?" He peered at me. "You're that actor that was in the picture with him."

"That's right," I said. It was gratifying to know I was almost famous at The Trade Winds. "Now, would you mind telling me why you roughed me up?"

He looked almost ashamed. "I thought you were the one . . . the one Robbie talked about."

"What one?"

"You know. The one who—hired him. The day he was killed."

"Why did you think that, for God's sake?"

Barry said, "Robbie told us he was an older guy, very good-looking. You fit the description."

I liked the part about very good-looking but wasn't too thrilled with the other half. I said, "What else did Robbie say?"

"He said the guy was driving a BMW."

I sighed. I was tiring of hearing about the BMW. "Is that all? I mean, can you remember anything else, even if you think it's nothing?"

"Robbie and Kevin came in that night. They were always fun to be around, because Robbie had such a great sense of humor. They were really devoted to each other, and I liked that. It's not that usual on this street, you know, and it kind of gave me hope that it might happen to me sometime. Anyway, we were all sitting at a table, and Robbie started telling us about this guy who had given him fifty bucks just to drive around and talk and was going to give him another hundred the next morning just for running an errand. He was pretty jazzed; he hated tricking. So he thought with that guy's hundred and fifty he could stay off the streets for a few days and concentrate on getting maybe another job as an extra in a movie."

"And he said the guy was older and good-looking? Did he happen to say how old? Thirty? Fifty?"

All at once Barry looked at me with suspicion. "Just why do *you* want to know?"

I gave him one of my cards. "That's what I was reaching for when you started playing handball with me."

"I'm sorry," he said, and squinted at the card. "'Investigations'? I thought you were an actor."

"I'm both," I said. "Kevin Brody asked me to help him find out what happened to Robbie. That's why I'm here."

Barry nodded acceptance. "What did you ask me again?"

"Did Robbie say how old the man was?"

"No, just older. But he couldn't have been past fifty."

"Why not?"

Barry smiled. "In the gay world they place a great premium on youth and beauty. That's my problem, I've got neither. But when Robbie said 'older' he probably meant somewhere around forty. If the guy had been fifty or more, Robbie would have said 'old.'"

That cleared Raymond Sheed again. I said, "Well, we're narrowing it down some."

"Look, Robbie didn't talk much about how he made his living. We all knew it, but it wasn't something he was terribly proud of. The reason he mentioned this at all is probably because he didn't have to—do anything. You know."

"Barry, you knew Robbie pretty well. Is there—was there—anyone in his life that I should know about? Anyone besides Kevin that he might have—"

"There was no one!" Barry thundered, or as close to thundering as he could come with that ridiculous voice. "I told you, he and Kevin loved each other."

I nodded.

He said, "Look, I want to help, I really do. I'd do just about anything I could to find this son of a bitch."

"You sound like a good friend to have, Barry."

He looked down at his shoes, and when he looked up there was something in his eyes very much like fear.

"It's not so much that, even though that's part of it. But— this just might be some loony who's decided he wants to kill off the entire homosexual population of Los Angeles. God knows which one of us could be next!"

5

At noon the next day I was walking into the lobby of Saint Ignatius Hospital in Santa Monica. I had called Steven Brandon at nine, explained my mission, and begged an audience. He'd said, "If you're trying to get a part in a movie I'm going to have you boiled in oil," but I'd assured him such was not the case, and he'd reluctantly agreed to see me. Probably several other out-of-work actors had tried to get into his room for the wrong reason, captive audience that he was, and I understood his caution.

A blue-suited young man stood guard outside his room. I was willing to bet he was one of the janissaries from the Triangle studio page staff pressed into special duty. They'd picked a big one. I told him my name and that I had a noon appointment, and he disappeared into the room, closing the door behind him, emerging a few minutes later to hold the door open for me.

Steven Brandon was sitting up in bed. The left side of his face and neck were bandaged, and his left arm and shoulder were encased in a formidable-looking cast. He was wearing silk pajama bottoms and soft leather slippers. It was obvious even though he was sitting down that he was a mere Munchkin of a man, not much taller than five two or five three, with sandy blond hair and twinkly blue eyes. There was a copy of *Variety* and the *Hollywood Reporter* on the blanket, along with an official-looking folder and three scripts. He motioned me to a chair at the side of the bed. "Sit on my right side," he said, "I can't hear much out of my left ear."

"I'm sorry," I said.

"That's okay. Most of what I have to listen to is bullshit anyway. What can I do for you?"

"I'm trying to find out what happened that morning."

"That's pretty common knowledge, isn't it?"

"Well, yes, but—"

"Look, get to the bottom line, okay?"

"Okay. Tell me about that morning. I mean, where the other car was, where you were, anything else you can remember."

"I've been through this with the police, the insurance company—Jesus Christ, I have a headache."

"I'm sorry, I'll try to be brief."

"That'll be nice."

I waited a moment, then prompted, "That morning?"

"Right. I was driving south down Cicada Drive. I stopped at the stop sign at the corner of Roscoemare, in the right-hand lane because I was going to turn right. On my left this kid comes driving up, stops beside me, gives the horn a little honk. So I turned around to look at him. He was leaning across the seat like he was going to roll down the window, so I started to roll down mine. I figured he wanted to ask directions or something."

"And then?"

He turned his right hand palm up. "*Ka-boom!* Next thing I knew I was right here in this bed with a headache very similar to the one I feel coming on now."

"You never saw this kid before?"

"I'd shake my head but it hurts to. No. I understand he was some kind of fairy."

"He was a homosexual."

"Didn't I say that?"

"Mr. Brandon, you live in Malibu, don't you?"

"Check."

"Would you mind telling me what you were doing on Cicada Drive at nine forty-five in the morning?"

He turned to look directly at me, his head somewhat lopsided from the bandages. The look in his eyes could have turned chicken soup into ice cubes. "Driving south," he said. He held my gaze with his own. I was sure he didn't want to pursue that particular line of inquiry.

"Did you see anything else? Anyone hanging around?"

"Look, I was driving along, minding my own business. I wasn't looking for assassins in the bushes."

"Maybe," I said, "you should have been."

"And exactly what is that supposed to mean?"

I shrugged. "I don't know. But from where I sit it looks as if Robbie Bingham was a guided missile sent to get you."

He blinked. "That is horse puckey!" he said.

"I hope so. But who would go to all that trouble just to blow up a bit actor?"

He leaned over toward me, and a green-covered script fell off the bed and onto the floor. He waited just a heartbeat for me to pick it up, and when I didn't he glared at me as if to say I'd never work another show at Triangle Broadcasting again. "Do you ever read the newspaper, Mr. Saxon? Besides *Variety,* I mean. There's a terrible epidemic going around: it's called AIDS, and it strikes largely in the gay community. Now if this little faggot had given someone a dose of—"

I stood up. "Robbie Bingham was a friend of mine, Mr. Brandon, and he's dead now. Watch your mouth."

Brandon looked stunned. It had probably been a long time since anyone had talked that way to him. He didn't seem angry or upset, simply disoriented, as though he were being addressed in an alien tongue. Finally he slumped back against the pillow and closed his eyes. "If you did an autopsy on the kid," he said, "you might find he was sick with AIDS."

"There weren't any pieces left of him big enough to do an autopsy on, Mr. Brandon."

"Saxon, this is a hospital. I wasn't feeling too great to begin with; the very reason I'm here. And you've made me feel considerably worse. So if you don't mind . . ."

"Can you think of anyone who wants you dead?"

His eyes opened. "Jesus, what are you saying?" he sputtered, then took a deep breath and composed himself. Steven Brandon was rarely at a loss for words, so I knew the idea had upset him gravely. He rubbed the end of his nose with his finger. "I don't know," he said. "You're in the business. You know you can't run a network without making a couple of enemies—more than a couple. I know lots of people that hate my guts. But enough to want to kill me? I don't think so."

"I'm not asking you to accuse anyone. Look, I have no official capacity, I'm just a friend. But it would be very helpful if you could come up with a few names."

He made a wry face. "Any producer whose show I canceled. Any actor whose pilot I didn't pick up. Anyone who might inherit my job when I die. My ex-wife. Twenty ex-lovers—or maybe two hundred, I don't know. My opposite numbers at the other networks. Tom Brokaw. The fucking Russians. How the hell do I know?" He shifted around in the bed. "That's a hell of a thing to ask somebody, you know that?"

"I didn't mean to spook you."

"Spook me? I damn near get blown to pieces and you tell me it might have been deliberate, and you don't want to *spook* me? Jesus Christ!"

"The police seem to think Robbie Bingham was the target and you were just an innocent victim."

"I'd like to think that, too, but now you've got me—"

"It was just a thought," I said.

"Look, Saxon, you're some kind of private cop, right?"

"Right," I said.

"And you're just doing this for a favor, this investigation?"

"I knew Robbie slightly. His—friend asked if I'd look into it."

"Are you getting paid?"

"I said I knew Robbie. This is for nothing."

He inserted a finger as far as he could get it into his cast at the neckline. "This itches like a bastard," he said. Then he looked at me. "I'll pay you three hundred a day to investigate this," he said. "Determine whether there's someone out to get me. If there is, find out who and tell the cops."

I started to say something but he rushed right on.

"Three hundred a day plus expenses, plus a bonus of a thousand if the guy is caught and put away. Plus I'll cut you a deal at the network. Personal services contract. Guarantee you a thousand a week for two years and x number of featured roles in movies of the week."

What I said next turned my guts to marinara sauce. "I'll take your money, Mr. Brandon, that's my business. As for the contract, well, I'd rather be hired on my merits as an actor. Thanks all the same." Look, I never said I was bright.

He stared at me a long time and then blew air through his front teeth. "Proud son of a bitch, aren't you?"

"I'd like to think so."

"Not too proud to take my money for what you were going to do for free anyway."

"Proud. Not stupid."

"No, I guess not."

"But if I accept your money I have to treat you like any other client, network or no network. Okay?"

"I suppose."

"And that means you have to give me as much as you can to work with so it'll make my job easier and help me to do what you want."

His eyes narrowed. "Saxon," he said, "guys ten times smarter than you come into my office every day and try to shmooze me. Heavyweight guys, like Aaron Spelling and Norman Lear and David Wolper. Most of the time I let 'em because they've got something I want. I'm not sure I'm going to let you."

"Then forget we ever had a conversation, Mr. Brandon," I said. "Thanks for your time." I walked around the bed and started for the door.

"Wait a minute, wait a minute, come back here," he said, and his tone was cajoling, not imperative, which is the only reason I did what he wanted me to. I stood by the side of the bed and he said, "Come on over here by my good ear," and as I walked around to the other side he muttered, "God damn it, the only people I ever hear say that are ninety-five fucking years old!"

When I was standing where he wanted me to, he said, "Are you always this much of a hardass? Probably why you don't get more work as an actor. It's okay to be hardassed when you're Newman or Redford. When you're Saxon . . ." He turned the palm of his good hand upward. "Okay," he said, "what do you want from me?"

"I want to know what you were doing on Cicada Drive in Beverly Hills at nine o'clock in the morning when your house is in Malibu and your office is in Burbank."

He reached for a plastic cup full of ice water and took a long swig. "You dirty son of a bitch," he said.

6

The house at 953 Cicada Drive was antebellum in design, as if they had shot some of the exteriors of *Gone With the Wind* there. Willow and magnolia trees lined the winding driveway, and the grass on the sweeping carpet of lawn was almost blue-green. The house itself was two stories, white, with a verandah running along the entire facade, the doorway framed by Doric columns. As I drove slowly toward the house I listened for the slaves singing in the fields, but they must have been on a coffee break. The only thing that didn't fit the rest of the picture was that the mistress of the manor herself came to the door to greet me.

Raina Stone in her prime had been one of the loveliest women ever to walk in front of a camera. Black-haired and blue-eyed, there was never a moment when her on-screen persona was not radiating sensuality, an exotic promise of delights far beyond the experience of the countless male movie fans who made her the reigning sex goddess, along with Marilyn Monroe, of the fifties. Monroe was the vulnerable innocent whose overwhelming sexiness seemed to be an afterthought; Raina Stone was the slut, the corrupter, the Mother Goddamn of the Eisenhower era who knew more than she'd ever tell and who held back nothing, the Susie Homewrecker doll who walked away from the wreckage laughing. Raina Stone in her early fifties was still drop-dead gorgeous and still promised delights. I was impressed as hell just to meet her.

"Steven said you'd be coming," she said as she led me through a cavernous entryway into a room with a skylight and two glass walls and more plants than I had ever seen before in a private home. Her voice was the product of too many cigarettes and too much liquor and drugs and an excess of an awful lot of other things that had been dutifully chronicled in the world press for almost thirty years. She was wearing a black peasant skirt and an off-the-shoulder white blouse and her hair was pulled back into a girlish ponytail. She was so beautiful that she almost got away with it. "I have no idea how I can help you, but we'll have a shot at it, shall we?"

She arranged herself artfully on a settee, giving me just a flash of thigh before spreading her full skirt around her knees. I sat on an upholstered straight-backed chair and politely declined her offer of a drink. I noticed she already had one on a table next to the settee, a tall glass filled with medium-brown liquid in which the ice cubes were practically melted. There was a wet Kleenex wrapped around the bottom of the glass. She took a healthy swallow from it and lit a cigarette and blew the smoke in my direction. It made me want one.

"Now, tell me what this is all about, if you will," she said. "I love intrigue. Back in the good old days this town was full of intrigue, baby. Who was trying to get out of their studio contract, who was fucking whom, who was a Communist. Today there are no studio contracts, everyone is fucking everyone else, and the town is full of Republicans."

"I'm not sure there *is* any intrigue, Miss Stone."

"Raina," she corrected. "Am I that goddamn old? Miss Stone is an old-maid librarian. Is that how I seem to you?"

"You seem the same to me as when you were in *The Stars at Night*," I said, paying her the compliment for which she had been fishing, and then I added, "Raina."

She laughed. "You're a lying sack of shit, but you have a certain charm," she said. "I like the gray hair; it's sexy. Do you remember Jeff Chandler?"

I nodded.

"His gray hair was sexy, too," she said. "Remember when he played that gray-haired Indian with Jimmy Stewart?"

"*Broken Arrow*," I said.

"Give the man a box of Snickers." A deep puff of smoke, and on the exhalation she said, "But you didn't come here to play Trivial Pursuit."

"No, I didn't, but if I could have a rain check?"

"In writing," she said. "So. Let's hear it."

"Mr. Brandon told me he had just left your house when he—had his accident."

"Mr. Brandon tells it true."

"I don't mean to pry, but—"

"Sure you do," she said cheerfully. "You want to know what he was doing here at nine o'clock in the morning. Well, I think you know. You look like a smart guy."

"Did he come here often?"

"In the past six months he's spent a lot of nights here, Mr. Saxon. Does that shock you?"

"Of course not."

"I mean the fact that I'm almost twenty years older than he is?"

"You're almost twenty years older than I am, and it wouldn't stop me."

"Gallantry. That's classy. You're a class act."

"It takes one to know one, Raina."

She threw back her head and guffawed. She was a lusty woman, there was no mistaking that. "No one ever accused me of having class," she said. "That's because I never banged the right people—like producers and directors and studio heads. Trumpet players, bullfighters, band singers were more my speed. But my salvation in this town was that I never gave a brown rat's ass what anyone thought of me except the people who bought the tickets and paid the freight. I owed them a performance and I always gave them one. I was no Katharine Hepburn, but they came to see the smoldering sexpot and I always delivered. Didn't I?"

"Always," I agreed.

"So I suppose you're wondering what I'm doing with a little pisher like Steven?"

"No, I—"

"It's not hard to figure out. When I was a kid just getting started in pictures I never bothered with big shots because I didn't want the feeling that anyone owned me. I got my jobs and my contracts because I was good at what I did on the screen, and I got my jollies from the earthier types. Even my two husbands were Italian. Now I'm with Steven because I don't want to cater to the star-fuckers, the semi-queens, the vultures that circle this town looking for almost-dead meat. He's rich and he's powerful and I don't want a goddamn thing from him because I'm retired from all that shit. I'm not going to play anyone's mother and I can't compete with the twenty-two-year-old dollies for the other roles. He makes me feel good and we each pay our own way and I like it like that. The energy he shows in running a network is the same kind of energy he shows me upstairs, and for an old broad that's not too bad. And he's with me not because I'm Raina Stone, aging sex goddess, but because I'm an E ticket, baby, still the best ride in the park. Yes, he spends three or four nights a week here, and nobody in this whole dirty town knows about it because he squires younger and more appropriate ladies to all the fancy parties and everyone thinks he's the big swinging bachelor around town, and for all I know he might be and I don't care as long as he comes home to momma as often as he does. Now, what else can I tell you?"

"You say no one knows about your relationship?"

"It's hardly common knowledge. We both agreed we didn't want to go public like Burt Reynolds and Dinah Shore because we didn't want the jokes and the crap they had to put up with. And because after thirty years I was damn tired of having it in the papers every time I dropped my panties. And because it's nobody's business."

"Then some people might know?"

"*You* know," she said.

"I know. The nights Mr. Brandon spent here, Raina; were they definite nights of the week, or was it kind of a random thing?"

She waved her cigarette at me. The spent ashes fell onto her skirt and she flicked them away aimlessly. "More random. I guess he kept Fridays and Saturdays to himself because he always had to go to some party or other. I never went with him. Why should I? I never went when I was a star."

"You're still a star."

She looked at me lewdly. "You don't know the half of it, kiddo." Another swallow; then she stood up and went to a portable bar near one of the windows and poured herself another drink. I saw from the bottle that it was rye she was drinking, with just a splash of water and a few ice cubes. "What's the difference what nights he was here?"

"If he followed a pattern—say, Mondays, Tuesdays, and Thursdays—then it's possible that someone knew it, knew he'd be at the corner of Cicada and Roscoemare at a certain time on a certain morning."

She came back to the settee with the full drink, and she was frowning. "You aren't saying that bomb was meant for Steven?"

"I'm keeping an open mind about it, but it might turn out that way, yes."

She smote her forehead and sat down. "Holy shit!" she said. "You mean someone wasted that kid just to get at Steven?"

"I don't know, Raina. That's what he's hired me to find out. I know he has lots of enemies because of his job. But is there anyone that you know of, anyone in *your* life, for instance, that might want him to get hurt?"

She became thoughtful, then rueful. "Twenty years ago,

sure, lots of guys would have killed for me. They sure as hell fought for me often enough. But now . . . Who'd kill over an old broad with a cigarette cough and drooping tits?"

"Who were you seeing before Steven? Six months ago."

"A Bolivian real estate tycoon who was sixty-seven years old and liked having a movie star around to amuse his buddies. His name was Simon de Uriarte, and I haven't seen him in about a year. Or heard from him, either, except a basket of gourmet Christmas candy in December. He wouldn't be the type to plant a bomb, mainly because he never gave enough of a shit. Besides, he spends most of his time in Bolivia. He owns about half of it anyway."

"Who are Steven Brandon's close friends?"

"Everybody in this town who wants to sell a show to Triangle. Which is another way of saying everybody in this town."

"No one special he hangs around with?"

"Well, there's Irv Pritkin; he's head of Triangle Daytime Programming. Stuart Wilson, runs the network's movie division. Sanda Schuyler, head of network development, and may I add the biggest bull dagger in the industry."

"A lesbian?"

"That's what they call them. Anyway, those are the three people Steven spends most of his time with. Besides his tennis pals, John McEnroe and Charlton Heston and Vince Van Patten. But he just sees them on the courts."

"If he plays with them, he must be pretty good."

"If Steven isn't good at something he doesn't do it at all," she said. "That's just the way he is. And that's why I let him spend so much time over here."

I stood up. "Raina, I really appreciate your taking the time to see me. You've not only been a big help, but it was a real thrill to meet you."

"It probably was." She came over to me, leaving her drink

on the table but carrying a newly ignited cigarette. "You should have met me twenty years ago, baby," she said. "There wouldn't have been a trace of you left except your shoes in a small puddle." She put her hand on the side of my face. It felt dry and rough. No matter how well a woman may age, her hands always seem to give her away, TV commercials notwithstanding. "Ever kiss a real movie star, kiddo? Ever kiss a fucking legend?"

Slowly, very slowly, as if the camera were rolling and moving in tight for a close-up, she brought her mouth to mine, and when I parted my lips she did things to my tongue with hers that I hadn't known about before, very nice things, very wicked and very exciting things. When I put my arms around her I could feel the extra layers of flesh that hadn't been there when she'd appeared opposite Robert Taylor and Stewart Granger and Gregory Peck. But it didn't matter a damn bit, because she was far and away the best kisser I'd ever run into, and she *was* a fucking legend, and I'll carry the memory of that kiss with me for a long, long time. Even after I'd driven away from the house on Cicada Drive and wiped off the excess lipstick with a tissue, my mouth still tingled from a world-class kiss.

7

When I got back to the office Jo was just getting ready to leave. She brought in a stack of messages for me, cocking a pert eyebrow. "Kevin Brody called twice," she said, "and someone named Barry. Is there something you'd like to tell me, as a friend?"

"No," I said, "there isn't. I haven't come out of the closet, if that's what you're implying."

"Just wondering," she said.

"If you ever decide to dump your husband, I'll prove it to you."

"Thanks anyway," she said, "but I gave at the office. How's the Bingham case coming?"

"That's the hell of it," I said, "I'm not sure if it is the Bingham case. It might be that Robbie was simply a human bomb sent after somebody else."

"Steven Brandon?"

"Could be?"

She shook her head. "Have you ever considered moving to someplace nice and quiet like Oklahoma City and doing insurance cases?"

"As a matter of fact I have," I said. "Oklahoma City looks mighty pretty."

She left, and I turned on the radio while I went through the pink While You Were Out slips. With the exception of calls from Kevin and Barry nothing seemed terribly urgent. Mike Campbell, one of my favorite jazz singers, had called to tell me he was doing two weeks at The Money Tree, a little jazz joint in Toluca Lake; the owner of the little wine shop near my apartment in Pacific Palisades wanted me to try a new wine he'd just gotten in; Jake McHargue, an actor buddy, had called to cancel golf that Saturday because he had to go out of town; Ray Tucek, a stuntman I often use in my cases when I needed muscle, had just wanted to say hello, nothing important—things like that. Before I did anything else I called Triangle Broadcasting and made appointments with the three people whose names I'd gotten from Raina Stone—Irv Pritkin, Sanda Schuyler, and Stu Wilson. Their secretaries were all properly protective, asking me what firm I was with, to which I replied Saxon Investigations, and whether the callee would know what this was in regard to, to which I answered that it would depend on his or her psychic powers, a smartass approach that would have done me little good had I not mentioned the magic name Steven Brandon immediately thereafter. I made three appointments for the next morning.

Then I called Kevin Brody at Delacort's.

"I hadn't heard from you," he said accusingly. "I got worried."

"I'm working on it. These things tend to go rather slowly at best."

"Look," he said, a catch in his voice, "I know Robbie was nothing to you, and being straight you might not comprehend what I'm saying, but he was the love of my life. We fall in love just like you do."

"I know that, Kevin."

"Hey, if it's the money, I can borrow—"

"It's not the money," I said. "I told you that before." I debated revealing my deal with Steven Brandon but thought better of it. Kevin was too emotional at this point to be rational. "I've been on this all day yesterday and today, and I have things scheduled for tomorrow. I'm not dragging my feet. I made a commitment to you and I always keep my word."

He paused. Then, "I'm sorry."

"I know how you feel," I said. "Believe me, I'm on top of it. Full time."

"Full time? What if your agent calls with a fat juicy part in a movie?"

"From your lips to God's ear," I said.

I called Barry Haworth.

"Thanks for calling back," he said in that ridiculous girlish voice. "Can you meet me at The Trade Winds tonight? About nine?"

"I guess so. Why?"

He sounded annoyed. "I'm not asking you for a date, for Christ's sake! There's somebody I want you to talk to. About Robbie."

"Can't you bring him to my office?" I said. "The Trade Winds isn't exactly my scene."

"Look, this kid's uptight enough about talking to heat."

"I'm not heat," I said, "just a private investigator."

"That's a fine line," he said. "Do you want to talk to this kid or not? He saw Robbie get into the BMW."

"I'll be there."

"And you're buying the drinks."

The Trade Winds hadn't improved much in twenty-four hours. I wore a turquoise sports shirt and white slacks so I wouldn't look quite as out of place as I had the previous night in a jacket and tie. It didn't help much. The guy who had asked me to dance the night before was there again. This time he was in white velour.

"Look who's back!" he said as he brushed by me carrying a beer. "Little Miss Stuck-up!"

I sighed. Oklahoma City was starting to sound like a viable option.

Barry's bulk made him hard to miss. We shook hands, and I noticed the discolored swelling under his eye, a Saxon souvenir. He saw me looking at it and smiled.

"It's okay," he said. "I deserved it. It's my knee that really hurts. I'm glad you could come."

I got a beer and we sat down at one of the ringside tables. A half finished drink and a pack of More Reds were at one of the places.

"As I mentioned," Barry said, "Jimmy is kind of nervous about this, so go easy." He brushed his fingers across the mouse on his cheekbone. "Curb your natural instincts."

"Need I point out that you started the rough stuff last night?"

He smiled. "How was I to know you're such an animal?"

We watched the dancers, and then the song ended and two young men came over to the table. One of them thanked the other and went off into the crowd. The one who sat down was rather grungy-looking, not far out of his teens, with a sprinkling of acne still on his cheeks. He had straw-colored hair and looked as though he should have been hanging around someplace in Ohio. He wore a bluish-gray windbreaker and tight blue jeans and a plaid shirt.

"Jimmy, this is the man I told you about; Mr. Saxon."

Jimmy and I shook hands, but I could tell his heart wasn't in it. He looked around nervously.

"Jimmy," I said, "anything you can tell me about Robbie Bingham's last day on the street would be tremendously helpful."

"Yeh," he said. That's all he said.

"I don't know if Barry's told you, but I'm not with the police. Anything you say to me will be kept in the strictest confidence."

He finished the drink on the table and looked around for a waiter. When one arrived he ordered a vodka and tonic.

"Do you want anything else?" I asked. "A sandwich or something?"

He shook his head. He nervously took one of the cigarettes

out of the pack and lit it, cupping his hands around the flaring match. I looked at Barry with some impatience.

"Let's wait until the waiter comes back," Barry said. Jimmy nodded his head, although it looked more like he was ducking a blow.

I paid for the drink when it arrived, and waited until Jimmy had taken a few gulps. He drank as though he were thirsty. I knew how he felt, and worked on my beer for a bit. The music was loud enough to make my ears hurt.

Finally I said, "You knew Robbie?"

"Yeh."

"Well?"

"I seen him around."

"Where?"

He sneered at me. "Where you think, man? On the street."

That stopped me. The idea of anyone paying to have sex with Jimmy was beyond my comprehension, but I noticed Barry shifting uncomfortably in his chair.

"I repeat, Jimmy, I'm not a policeman. All I want to do is find out about Robbie."

"So?"

"Barry says you might know something."

"Yeh."

I took out a twenty-dollar bill and pushed it across the table at him. He pushed it back. "You wanna trick with me, it costs more than that," he said. "Otherwise, put your fucking money in your pocket."

I did.

"Whattaya wanna know?"

"Anything you can tell me about Robbie and the BMW."

"Usually I don't pay attention to anything that goes down with other guys," he said. "I got enough trouble making a buck myself. But I'd just tricked with some guy in a red Chevy—you know the type, straight, fat, short-sleeved shirt with pencils in the pocket. The curious type. Anyways, he wanted to get me out of his car as fast as he could in case anybody that he knew saw him. So he let me off right near Santa Monica and Garden. Usually I work further down toward Vine Street. I figured I'd grab some lunch at the Casa."

"This was lunchtime, then?"

"Yeh. So I'm walking down the street—"

"Which side?"

"Huh?"

"Which side of the street?"

"Um . . . this one. The north side. And I seen Robbie across the street and I kinda waved, you know, 'cause I seen him around. And he waved back. And then this BMW pulls up alongside him and he leans over talking to the guy through the window."

"On the passenger side?"

"Yeh. Right. And after a second or two he gets into the car and off they go. I only remember on account of I thought Robbie had himself a spender. Probably good for at least thirty-five bucks for head."

"Did you get a good look at the driver?"

He shrugged again. "Naw, he had his face turned away from me. He was talkin' to Robbie. Besides, he was wearing sunglasses."

"Did you see *anything*?"

He finished his drink and I signaled for another round. Jimmy said, "Gray hair, expensive haircut. I think a mustache but I'm not sure."

"How can you not be sure about a mustache?"

"Look, man, I wasn't really paying that much attention, you know? I've seen Robbie get into a hundred cars, and every other guy on the street, too. That's what we do. I don't take notes or anything."

"But you think the man might have had a mustache?"

"Yeh."

Silence. Then, "So the next day when I heard that Robbie got snuffed, I flashed back on it."

"Why didn't you go to the police?"

"What are you, fuckin' crazy, man?"

I guess I was.

"Look, that's all I know, okay? I didn't get the license number of the car or nothin'."

"You remember what color it was? What the man was wearing?"

He shrugged again. "The car was dark-colored—black or maroon or dark blue. Who the fuck remembers?"

"And what was the guy wearing?"

"I dunno. Dark suit and tie, I guess."

"Anything else you can tell me, even the smallest detail?"

He shook his head and frowned into the smoke ring he'd just blown. Then he said, "Oh, yeh, I noticed one thing."

I leaned forward.

"The car needed washing. It was kinda dusty, like it was parked outside most of the time."

I finished my beer. "Jimmy, I appreciate your talking to me. Is there anything I can do for you?"

He laughed, but he didn't seem very amused. "Not a thing. I'm in Fat City—can't you tell?"

I shook his hand, left a few dollars on the table for the waiter, and started for the door. Barry followed and stopped me.

"Look," he said, "please don't think badly of me, okay?"

"Why should I think badly of you? You've helped me."

He looked back at the table. Jimmy was being asked to dance. "Because of him. And me. I'm an overweight, aging queen, Mr. Saxon, and funny-looking to boot. Most of the time if I want sex, I have to buy it. Jimmy is—"

I put my hand on his elbow. "Barry, what you do is your

business. I think you're a pretty nice guy, if it means anything."

It was hard to tell in the dim light, but I think his eyes got misty. "It means a lot. You'll never know." And then he hugged me, his hairy cheek next to mine. By the time I got my composure back he'd worked his way back into the crowd.

Near the door I ran into the guy with the white velour shirt. "Leaving so soon?" he said.

"Afraid so."

"Couldn't find anything to suit your exquisite tastes?"

I didn't answer him. I tried to keep moving but he planted himself directly in front of me.

"I just want you to know I'm on to you, Mary." He was quivering with indignation. "You're a married straight, curious as hell, starting to question yourself, so you come around here and check things out every night, but you don't have the balls to do anything because you're afraid to go home to little wifey with cockbreath. Am I right or wrong?"

"Your insight is fabulous," I said.

"Well, when you finally come out of the closet, don't come sniffing around me. I wouldn't have the best part of you. You're too fucking old!" He flounced away, obviously feeling much better.

I had arrived at the nightclub early enough to have found a space in the miniature parking lot next to the building and I was grateful I didn't have to walk very far. I got into my car and carefully edged it out of its slip in the lot and out onto the street, heading west down Santa Monica Boulevard to my digs in the far-off Palisades. I wasn't too sure how I felt about the velour shirt telling me I was too old, either. I wanted very much to get home.

As I approached Fairfax Avenue I noticed a gray Rams T-shirt among all the other male humanity on the sidewalk. It was Marvel, standing up against a building and talking to a white man in his late twenties, and the conversation, at least on the man's part, seemed to be very animated, if not heated. I slowed down for a better look, just in time to see the white man slap Marvel across the face very hard. Marvel didn't seem disposed to retaliate, and the man did it again, this time with the back of his hand. Marvel's head rolled from side to side as though held to his shoulders by a rubber band. I braked to a stop and leaned over the passenger seat toward the two. The top was down so I didn't even have to crank open a window.

"Marvel!" I called. The two of them turned and looked over at me. Marvel was crying.

"Just roll on down the road, pal, this is a private conversation," the white man said. He was pasty-faced, with too long blond hair and an earring in his right ear.

I ignored him. "Marvel, are you all right?"

"Are you fucking deaf?" Pasty Face said. "Take off!"

Marvel was cowering against the building. I got out and walked around the front of the car and onto the sidewalk. Angry drivers behind me were honking, swearing, and pulling around into the other lane to get by my car. Pasty Face took a few steps to meet me as I stepped up onto the curb.

"What's your act, cocksucker?" he said. "Take a walk."

"What's *your* act, cocksucker?" I said. "Why are you hitting the kid?"

"I'll do whatever I want to the kid. He belongs to me. Now get lost."

It was beginning to dawn on me that *take off, take a walk, get lost,* and *roll on down the road* meant that Pasty Face wanted me to go away. He should have asked me nicer.

"Marvel is a friend of mine," I said. "I don't like seeing him get pushed around."

"You wanna take his place, fag?"

Marvel was almost hysterical with fear. "It be okay. You go on. You hurt him, he gonna give me a beating."

"Nobody's going to beat you, Marvel. Get in my car."

I couldn't believe I'd said that. Looking back on it, I still can't believe it.

Marvel didn't move. I said, "Go on, it's all right."

Instantly there was a switchblade knife in Pasty Face's hand, pointing in the general vicinity of my rib cage. "I'll say what's all right," he told me. "You got more balls than brains. I'm gonna cut 'em off for you, faggot!"

I jammed my right thumb into his eye, and even before the scream came out of him I'd slashed my left hand down across his right wrist and the knife clattered to the sidewalk. I grabbed his now empty hand and twisted it up behind him in a hammerlock and shoved him face first into the side of the building. The crunch his nose made against the brick was a satisfying sound. His knees buckled and I gave an upward twist to his imprisoned arm and he rose up on his tiptoes, making a noise that sounded like *Nnnnnnnnh* sung in E above high C. Over my shoulder I said, "Get in the car, Marvel. Now!"

The frightened boy got into my car, and I increased the pressure on Pasty Face's arm, changing the consonant sound he had been making into a more open vowel sound, a kind of bubbly moan, coming as it did through his bleeding nose. "Okay, it's all over, punk," I said. "Let it go now or I'll tear your arm off." I moved him about six inches away from the wall and then slammed him into it again. This time he took the impact on the side of his face. I grabbed the back of his neck, his hair greasy under my fingers, and squeezed, forcing him down to his knees. "All the way," I said, and he lay down on his face on the sidewalk. I decreased the pressure on his arm and bent over him and said softly, "You're going to stay right here until we're gone; if you get up before that I'm going to give you a beating you'll never get over. Understand?" And I gave his arm another upward tweak, and this time he screamed.

I let go of his arm and neck and went back around to the driver's side of the car, not exactly running but moving quickly. I put the car in gear, causing the driver behind me to jam on his brakes and, I'm sure, call me an unkind name. At the next corner I turned right, wanting to get out of the heavy congestion of Santa Monica Boulevard. I went north to Fountain Avenue, a darker and less traveled street, and then headed west again, moving along at about twenty miles over the posted speed limit. Only then did I turn to look at Marvel, who appeared absolutely terrified.

"It's okay, Marvel. No one is going to hurt you anymore." He didn't answer, but I could see tears streaming down his cheeks. I couldn't tell if they were tears of uncertainty as to what was going to become of him or of relief to be out of a situation he obviously couldn't handle. It didn't matter.

At that hour the traffic between Hollywood and Pacific Palisades was minimal; most of the people who worked inland and lived by the ocean had already gone home, leaving the streets relatively uncongested. It took me about half an hour to make the drive, and during the trip conversation with Marvel was limited.

"Who was that guy?"

"That Tony."

"Is he your pimp?"

Marvel didn't say anything.

"Look, Marvel, I think I'm entitled to know what I'm in the middle of here."

He still didn't reply. He was staring, terrified, straight ahead. It's hard to keep your eyes open that wide in a convertible going fifty miles an hour, but he managed. I didn't push him with any more questions.

I got to my apartment and gave Marvel the guided tour. He kept saying "Oh, man" at each new wonder, like the blender and the microwave and the coffee mill and the dimmer

switches and the expensive stereo. My place was far from luxurious, but to Marvel it was some sort of fairyland, no pun
intended. I let him wander around pushing buttons until he
tired of it.

The tough part was explaining to Marvel that he was going
to be all right, that I wasn't going to put him out on the street
again, and especially that I didn't want to have sex with him.
It was almost as if he understood some of the things I said
and not others. In any case, conditioning had taught him to
perceive himself as a piece of meat to be used by everyone
and anyone in whatever fashion they desired, and although I
tried to assure him of his intrinsic worth as a human being I
realized that philosophically as well as emotionally this all
might be just a bit too much for him. So I gave him a Pepsi
and sent him off to take a shower.

I gave him my only pair of pajamas. I'm not a pajama
wearer and never have been, and these black silky numbers
had been given to me by an old lover whose desire to change
my habits had not stopped with sleepwear. They were big
enough for two of Marvel, and he kept rubbing them, enjoying the feel of them next to his skin. He was very much like a
small boy on Christmas morning. He didn't say much and
only answered once in a while when he was spoken to, but
after about an hour the fear and suspicion in his eyes was
almost gone, along with the tense set of his jaw whenever he
looked at me.

I salvaged one of the pillows from my bed and tossed it
onto the sofa in the living room with a spare blanket. And
then I put Marvel to bed, poured myself a generous jolt of
neat Laphroaig, turned on KKGO softly so as not to wake my
houseguest, and listened to the syrupy tones of nightside disc
jockey Chuck Niles as he whispered the intro to a George
Shearing cut. I was in my favorite chair, most of the lights in
the apartment were off, and I was feeling drained and achy

and too tired and hassled to think about my case the way I should have. I thumbed through my notebook, but all my jottings did not add up to any sort of recognizable pattern. Maybe things would begin to fall together tomorrow when I talked to the Triangle executives.

It wasn't until I had nearly finished my drink that the realization hit me: in my bed at that very moment was a seemingly simpleminded, underage, black homosexual prostitute, and I had no idea what I was going to do about him. I finished the drink and felt it kick in, and relaxed some of the muscles that were doing the carioca in my neck. Tomorrow, I thought. I'll think about that tomorrow.

8

It was a few minutes after eight in the morning. I was drinking my second cup of coffee and talking to my assistant over the phone; Marvel was in the living room watching a cartoon show on TV, working on his third English muffin and his third glass of milk. A cozy little domestic scene. I was trying to explain to Jo *why* Marvel was now living in my apartment, and entreating her to find someone who knew about where to put street kids. She was trying to explain to me that grown-up, mature adults just didn't act in an impulsive manner the way I did, and she was terribly worried as to what people were going to think, and then she wanted to know what in hell *I* had been thinking of when I'd plucked Marvel off the street. "Do you have any idea how many teenage hookers of both sexes were probably beaten up by their pimps last night?" she said. "I'm surprised you have any room left at your place."

"Jo, sometimes you've got to decide whether you're really in the game or you're just going to be a spectator."

She was quiet for a minute, and then she said, "Sorry, that was a shitty thing to say, and of course you're right. I'll make a couple of phone calls and see what we can do about this."

"That's my girl. There have to be several organizations that deal with runaways. But I wonder if we can't do better than that, get him placed in a school somewhere. I don't want him back out on the street. If that pimp doesn't find him and half kill him, some wierdo trick is going to."

"I'll take care of it. You're at Triangle all morning?"

"Yeah," I said, "but I'll be checking in. Thanks, Jo."

Marvel was so engrossed in his cartoons that I hated to disturb him, but I waited until a commercial for some grotesque humanoid dolls came on and gave him ten bucks in case he needed anything and told him where the nearest 7-Eleven store was located, and I even gave him an extra set of keys for the apartment. I wasn't sure he'd heard a word that I'd said because Bullwinkle and Rocky were commanding a lot more of his attention than I possibly could. I don't know why I wasn't uneasy about leaving him alone in my apartment. After all, I didn't even know the kid. But I had all my cash with me, my camera was fairly well hidden, I had a very old stereo, and I never watched television anyway, so I had little to lose if he decided to clean me out. Besides, there was just something about him that made me know he'd be there when I got home.

The same bloat-bellied guard checked me in at Triangle, and it gratified me to know there was someone whose working hours were as lousy as mine. I parked as close to the entrance as I could, and as I walked through the executive parking lot I noticed the majority of cars moored there were either Mercedes or BMWs, and most of them were dark in color. Because they spent a good bit of time in the outside lot, hard by the busy Ventura Freeway, almost all of them wore a thin film of dust. Not much help here.

I got another third degree from a security guard at the door, making me wonder what Triangle thought they had worth stealing. They kept no nuclear materials on hand, no defense secrets, and employed no Nobel laureates who put their research notes into shredders each night. Maybe they were jealously guarding the plans for their newest half-wit game show. In any event, they tried very hard to keep the public out, to keep their little enclave exclusive and mysterious and special, as did all the other TV and film facilities in Hollywood. All part of the grand illusion that it meant something.

I finally got up to the third floor, which was upper-management row at Triangle. I'd only been up there a few times before, and although it didn't seem like such a big deal to me, it seemed to impress hell out of those who worked there. Even the secretaries on this level were better-looking, classier, and they lorded it over the other secretaries because their bosses had more status at the network. It didn't seem to make any sense to me, but little about Hollywood makes much sense to me.

Irving Pritkin had a pretty secretary and a large corner office on the third floor, with his name on the door over the title VICE PRESIDENT—DAYTIME PROGRAMMING, and I guess that made him somebody. You sure couldn't tell by looking at him.

Pritkin was an accountant. It's what he'd wanted to be, what he'd studied for at UC–Santa Barbara, and what he was good at. When he was hired, the network had a policy that put their young executives through a rigorous year-long training program in which they spent a few weeks in every phase of network operations as assistants, thereby enabling them to learn as much as they could about TV networks. It had been Irv Pritkin's kismet to be in the daytime programming section at the time when the former VP had resigned, and in their wisdom the network mavens had elevated the assistant to the post of vice president, even though he had only been in daytime for three weeks and wouldn't have known a great game show or soap opera idea had it jumped up and bitten him on the ass. This was the man, however, who now held the fates of all producers of talk shows, game shows, and daytime dramas in his slim white hands. He had been on the job almost a year now, and he spoke importantly of his responsibilities.

"Did you know," he asked me in his reedy accountant's voice, "that daytime programming is responsible for thirty-seven percent of Triangle's overall advertising revenue?"

"No, actually, I didn't," I said. I glanced at the photographs on the office walls, each of them a daytime personality from the Triangle lineup, game show hosts like Tom Kennedy and Jim Peck and Scott Raney, and some of the stars of their number-two-in-the-nation soap opera, "Night Unto Night." I was sure that if the shows were canceled these photographs would disappear overnight.

"Steven Brandon started out in daytime, you know," Pritkin said as though he were explaining to me that my aged receivables were outweighing my accounts payable or something. "Most of the top network guys started with daytime: Bud Grant at CBS, Freddie Silverman. It's a hell of a learning experience. I know I learn something every day." Pritkin was an earnest, myopic, pear-shaped man who looked as if he never went out in the sun. He was fighting a losing battle with his hairline and his hips, trying to stop the retreat of one and the advance of the other. On his desk were photos of a pleasant-looking woman and two homely kids in White Sox Little League uniforms.

"How long ago was Steven Brandon in this department?"

"About five years back. Long before I ever got here. He went from daytime to nighttime long-form development to head of movies and miniseries, and then he took over as programming chief about three years ago." He recited these facts the way one might the facts of familiar history: *He started as a sportscaster in southern Illinois, then became a Hollywood star in the forties, served as president of the Screen Actors Guild, was the host of G.E. Theater, then became governor of California. After that . . .*

". . . The year after Steven took command," Pritkin went on, as though talking about General Patton, "we went from being a distant fourth network to being number two, and this year"—and he took a deep breath, as though the extra air would add import to what he was saying—"we've got a good shot at being number one." He held up one quivering finger. "If 'Streets of the City' continues to hold Tuesdays for us. I'm damn proud of that."

"So Steve Brandon must be a pretty popular guy around here?"

"Steven," he corrected, "everyone calls him Steven. I'd say that was an understatement. He's a hero, almost a cult figure."

"Over at the other three networks he must be like a bad dream. He's knocking their brains out."

Pritkin fiddled with his tie. He wore a blue dress shirt with a white collar, a discreet tie carefully knotted beneath his chin. His suit jacket was hung neatly on a hanger behind the door. His manicured nails only drew attention to his small hands. He said, "You are, of course, aware of what a cutthroat business this really is. Millions of dollars won or lost by the flip of a dial. You become a power when you learn what those people out there in television land really want."

I hadn't thought anyone said *television land* anymore except Lawrence Welk, which shows you how wrong I can be sometimes.

"And since Steven is obviously a power in this town, I suppose he's made some enemies, if I'm getting your drift," Pritkin said.

"You are."

"But I hardly think anyone here at Triangle would want to hurt him. He's our fearless leader, for God's sake."

"Never heard of anyone not liking their boss?"

"Steven isn't anyone's 'boss,' in that sense of the word, except maybe his secretary's. He's the big boss, and that makes it okay for people to like him here."

"What about the other networks?"

"Are you suggesting somebody from ABC or CBS tried to kill Steven Brandon because he's getting better ratings than they? Look, Mr. Saxon, this is an up-and-down business; it may be their turn in the barrel next season, and they know that."

"Mr. Pritkin, you're known around town as Steven Brandon's boy."

Owlish, he blinked. "Pardon me?"

"You're Steven's protégé, aren't you? I mean, didn't I hear someplace that when the vice presidency opened up it was basically Steven who railroaded your promotion through?"

Pritkin nodded. "Does that make me a suspect?"

"Just the opposite, I'd think."

"Well, I would, too." He touched his thinning hair—he didn't pat it or brush it or run his fingers through it; he touched it. "I'd lay down in front of a train for Steven Brandon. He gave me my career. I certainly wouldn't want to hurt him for it. I think you're out of sync on this one, Mr. Saxon. It's obvious someone was after that unfortunate young man in the other car and Steven Brandon was just an innocent victim."

"You and Brandon are pretty good friends?"

"I just told you, I owe my—"

"Do you know what he was doing on Cicada Drive that morning?"

Pritkin fidgeted. "Personal business, I suppose."

"How personal?"

"Too damn personal to discuss it with a stranger."

"Don't get testy, Mr. Pritkin. I happen to know what Brandon was doing there. I just wondered if you did."

He ducked his head as if avoiding a quick left jab. "It's not exactly common knowledge," he said, "but yes, I do know. Steven and I are fairly close, as I've said." He touched his hair again. "Why do you ask?"

"It's my job to ask questions."

"Maybe you ought to emcee one of our game shows."

"I'm available; Call my agent," I said, a little bit of my soul dying at the very thought. "Would you do me a favor, Mr. Pritkin?"

"If I can."

"You can. Would you take off your glasses?"

He laughed, a high-pitched whinny. "I'm stone blind without them."

"Just for a moment."

He took off his glasses and squinted in my general direction. The lenses were bottle-thick. "How's this?"

"Fine," I said, "thank you. I appreciate your cooperation, Mr. Pritkin."

He put his glasses back on, blinking and squinting again as his eyes readjusted. "What was that all about?"

"Worn glasses for a long time?"

"Ever since I was eight. I was the one they called Four-Eyes. Why?"

"I need them myself," I lied, standing up. "Trying to decide between glasses and contacts." He didn't believe me—I could tell by the way he shook my hand: it was one of those dead-fish handshakes.

I walked out into the busy corridor outside his office. There had been a deep red indentation on either side of his nose. Irv Pritkin had not been the man who'd rented the Ford Escort.

With twenty minutes to spare I decided to chance a trip to the infamous Triangle cafeteria, where I purchased a diet soda in a waxed cup and sat down at a table overlooking the BMWs in the parking lot.

"Hey there, fella, how are you?" Scott Raney was bearing down on me, a tray of evil meat loaf in his hands. "Mind if I join you?"

"Sit down," I said. He was wearing the toothpaste smile millions of housewives saw every day. I wondered if it ever turned off, if the mellifluous bass viol of a voice ever became

soft and intimate, or whether at the moment of orgasm he
cried out, "Tell her what she's won, Bill!"

He removed his lunch from the tray, using the tips of his
fingers. "Where'd you run off to the other night? I wanted to
introduce you to the crowd."

"I couldn't hang around," I said. "I'll have to catch the
show some other time."

"Just let me know when you're coming, okay, Hoot?"

He shouldn't have done that to me when I had a mouthful
of soda. It came shooting through my nose and I sputtered
and gagged.

"Easy, big fella," he said. What an asshole!

I got myself under control at last. A little piece of wax from
the cup had come off on my tongue, and I debated whether
to remove it daintily with my fingers or to spit it out. I chose
the second option—no one was looking.

"Did you see the numbers?" Scott Raney was saying. "The
new rating book? We took our time slot again. Seventeenth
week in a row."

"I'm so pleased for you," I said. "I guess that makes Steven
Brandon pretty happy, huh?"

The smile dimmed. It was nearly imperceptible, but if you
were really looking you noticed it. "Oh, fuck that little son of
a bitch," he said. He opened a bottle of Perrier that he'd obviously brought with him from home and poured it over the
shaved ice in his own waxed cup. "Brandon is in contract
negotiations with my agent at the moment, and I'm afraid he's
being a bit intractable."

"That doesn't seem fair," I said, "after you took your time
slot seventeen weeks running."

"That's how I look at it! You'd think he was playing with
his own money, for God's sake! He squeezes the buffalo so
hard it shits."

"Sounds like he's not your favorite guy."

Scott Raney's smile stretched as wide as he could possibly force it. "That's business. Personally, he's a really good buddy of mine. A very dear man."

"Rough what happened to him, the bomb and all."

He frowned as if an Iowa housewife had just missed the big bonus question and lost the trip to Puerta Vallarta. "That was an accident. I mean, I think they were trying to get the kid in the other car. But Steven's a pussycat, doesn't have an enemy in the world."

"Thirty seconds ago he was a son of a bitch."

"Hey! Everyone in this town is a son of a bitch, or else they'd go someplace else and be a ribbon clerk." He put a reassuring hand on my arm. "Not you, Hoot. I've never heard a discouraging word about you in this town. You and Jack Benny and Nat King Cole. Everyone loves you guys."

He began eating his meat loaf as though it were Chateaubriand, smacking his lips and chewing ostentatiously. His cheeriness was relentless, and it made my teeth ache as he prattled on about the good and bad points of working for Mark Goodson and Merrill Heatter and Bob Stewart. I found myself checking my watch. The cavalry arrived, however, as my friend Jay Dean wandered in for a cup of coffee and came over to the table to rescue me.

"Got a memo about you this morning," Jay said as he sat down across from me, ignoring his seventeen-weeks-in-a-row daytime star. "Says all staff members are to cooperate with you whenever possible and that you have the run of the lot. What's up?"

Scott Raney looked up, dabbing his lips daintily with a paper napkin. "When people start talking business, Scott Raney takes a cab. It's not my thing, you know? Great seeing you again, Hoot. Keep in touch, will you?" And, clapping me manfully on the shoulder, he strode off to Makeup and beyond, to the world of brand-new Buicks and a year's supply of Turtle Wax.

Jay looked after him. "Did he call you Hoot?"

"Yes," I said. I am just perverse enough that I didn't bother clarifying. Jay is one of those middle-management people that manage to survive the network wars by never demanding explanations from anyone, so I knew he'd just file it away for possible future use.

"You're working on the Brandon thing, aren't you? Is that why you were here the other night?"

"The kid who got killed in the explosion was a friend," I said. I didn't tell him Brandon had hired me.

"You're not going to learn much here," he said.

"Why not?"

"Because everyone loves Steven and is rooting for him to get better. Before he got here we used to lie about where we worked. Told people we sold storm doors. This network was the butt of a hundred jokes, like, 'You want to end the war in Vietnam? Put it on Triangle—it'll be finished in thirteen weeks.'"

"I remember," I said.

"Now we can hold our heads up. We're winners. We're a *factor*. This is the Brandon Era."

"For Christ's sake, Jay—"

"No, I'm serious. He's part of our pop culture now, like an astronaut or a rock star or a running back. The Miracle Worker."

"That was Helen Keller's friend."

"Was. Now it's Steven Brandon. He's turned this network around."

"Do you all kiss his ring each morning?"

Jay laughed and sipped his coffee. "I don't think he even knows my name," he said. "I'm just a cog in the wheel."

I looked at my watch. I had five minutes till my next appointment. "Tell me about Sanda Schuyler."

His eyes twinkled. "I think I'll let you find out for yourself."

"I'd heard some things."

"They're all true and in spades," he said. "But she's damn good at her job, and Steven trusts her. An awful lot of what's good around Triangle has come from Sanda—through Steven, of course."

"They're good friends?"

Jay began stuffing tobacco into a briar pipe. He's the most judicious man I've ever known, and his pipe-filling ploy frequently gave him a few extra seconds to think. "They have different life-styles, you know? I think they like and respect each other; that's about as far as I'll go."

I waved away the haze of blue smoke he blew at me. It only made me more keenly aware that I hadn't had a cigarette in forty-one days and change. His tobacco smelled like cherries. "Well, I guess I'll go pay a call on Ms. Schuyler. And don't worry, Jay, I promise not to hit her."

"You'd better not," he said. "She'd kick the shit out of you."

Back up on the third floor I found Sanda Schuyler's office. Her secretary was a slim, stunning black woman wearing a black-and-white dress and an expensive wedding ring. "Ms. Schuyler's expecting you, Mr. Saxon. Won't you go right in?"

Sanda Schuyler stood up as I approached her desk and stuck out her hand for me to shake. She was in her late thirties and her hair was cut short, mannish. It was flecked with gray, although not nearly as much as mine. She was tall, and I couldn't tell whether the breadth of shoulders was all her own or was built in to the blue suit she was wearing. She wore tinted glasses, aviator style, and was what is often referred to as "a handsome woman."

"Mr. Saxon, hello," she said. She spoke in a rather rapid staccato, the way Walter Winchell used to, except her voice was lower. "Please sit down. I've been looking forward to talking with you ever since Steven phoned me yesterday. Can I have Cheri bring you coffee?"

For a moment I was jealous. I guess you have to be a network biggie to have a secretary who brought coffee.

"No, thank you," I said, "I'm a bit of a coffee-holic and I've already had too much this morning."

"Aha-ha," she said. She sat down behind her desk and leaned back in her high-backed executive chair. She crossed her legs, and I had a quick, tantalizing peek up her skirt between her knees. "Of course, Steven told me why you were coming," she said, "and I'm afraid I can't be of any help at all. You should be digging into the life of that poor boy who was killed. I think Steven was a coincidental victim."

"Everybody seems to think that," I told her.

"How many times do you have to hear it before you start believing it?" She smiled, which took a little of the bite out of the question.

"I've never made a nickel in my business by accepting the obvious, Ms. Schuyler."

"Sanda," she said, and waited for me to correct myself.

"Sanda."

"I can make up something, if you'd like me to."

"No, I wouldn't like that at all."

"Then I repeat, I can't be of much help. Everyone I know likes Steven Brandon very much. Including me."

"Tell me a little about your job," I said.

"Why?"

"Curious, that's all."

Some of the pleasantness fell away, like fall leaves in a gust of wind. "I don't have time to satisfy your curiosity. I'm very busy."

"With what? That was my question."

"The sign on the door says Program Development."

"What's that?"

She looked at me narrowly, then took a cigarette out of a wooden box on the table and lit it with a plain silver lighter. Her fingernails were manicured but short, and though buffed to a sheen I could tell they were polishless. "You're an actor," she said. "You know damn well what it is."

"Hey, us actors only get to see casting directors. We don't know what goes on up here in the rarified atmosphere."

"All right, Steven said to humor you. People—producers, studios, writers—bring me an idea for a series. It's good, let's say, but not all there yet. I play with it, send them back to do more work, change a little here, shift a little there, get it so it's just the way I think it ought to be. Then I bring it to Steven and he makes a decision on it."

"Did you do that with 'Streets of the City'?" I asked.

"Why that show specifically?"

I shrugged.

"I did it with everything that's gotten on the air on this network for the last five years," she said. "And a hell of a lot that *didn't* get on the air."

"Fascinating. In other words, when you get interested in a project you work on it before Steven Brandon ever gets involved?"

"Right."

"And if he gives it a thumbs-down all your work is for nothing."

The gray-tinted glasses made it difficult to see her eyes. She blew some more smoke at me and I tried to inhale it surreptitiously. Secondhand smoking was better than no smoking at all.

"And you think I wanted to kill him because of that?"

"Whoa! No one said you tried to kill him."

"No one had to."

"As a matter of fact," I said, lying through my teeth, "I was thinking of one of those poor bastards who creates a show concept, gets all jazzed about it, gets *you* all excited about it, and then Brandon shoots it down."

"So you think Aaron Spelling did it?"

Even I had to laugh at that one.

"Are you a baseball fan?" she asked.

"I'm a baseball freak. Been a Dodger fan ever since I can remember. Why?"

"Take a great hitter: Pete Rose, Don Mattingly, Tony Gwynn. They generally hit up in the three hundreds somewhere, right?"

"Sure, on a good year."

"That means that about seven out of ten times they make an out."

"That's the way it works."

"How many of them do you suppose try to kill the opposing pitcher?"

"That's too easy," I said. "When you're investigating a murder you look everywhere, suspect everyone. It's not paranoia, it's just doing your job."

"Speaking of jobs," she said, "I have to get back to mine. Was there something else you wanted to ask me?"

"Where did you work before coming to Triangle?"

She smiled. "At a Dairy Queen in Madison, Wisconsin."

"Pardon me?"

"I worked my way through college at the Dairy Queen just off the University of Wisconsin campus," she said. "Then I came to California with a brand-new degree and got a job with Triangle Broadcasting. I've been here ever since."

"You must like it."

"I love it. And I love making it in a male-dominated business like this, too, without having to compromise myself or my integrity to do it."

"Is that how you got interested in baseball? So you could hold your own in a male-dominated—"

"Bullshit. I got interested in baseball because I grew up not far from where the old Milwaukee Braves played and my father used to take me. Eddie Mathews. Andy Pafko. Spahn and Sain and Pray for Rain—"

"Okay, okay, I believe you. We should take in a Dodger game some time."

"Why? What are you fishing for?"

"I don't follow."

"Look, Saxon, when Steven asked me to talk to you I did some phoning around. I know your reputation. You're smart and you do your homework."

"So? What's that got to do with the Dodgers?"

"You know damn well that I don't date men."

"Who said anything about a date? I just said a ball game; that doesn't mean we're going to pick out a silver pattern."

She stood up abruptly and gave me her firm, hearty handshake again. "You're wasting your time here," she said. "I'd be talking to the people in Boys Town about the bombing. It had nothing to do with Steven."

"Does the name Raina Stone mean anything to you?"

"Movie star in the fifties and sixties. Steven's overnighter. A lot of people's overnighter, at one time. When she first hit Hollywood they used to call her the Los Angeles Open."

"You don't think she'd have any reason to want Steven out of the way?"

"The way I heard it," Sanda Schuyler said, "the killer was a man."

"Isn't that always the way," I said, "in a male-dominated field like murder?"

9

Stu Wilson was a bluff, gruff man, well over six feet tall, with snow white hair done in a drill-sergeant buzz cut, and his manner fit his image. As head of the successful Movie of the Week division of the network, it was Wilson who was responsible for the long line of two-hour stories about wife-beating, child-molesting, parent-abusing, and a whole string of exotic diseases and disabilities that seemed to be the staple of long-form network television. It was he, in fact, who had developed and ramrodded *The Calico Cat,* the TV film in which I had appeared with Robbie Bingham. That one had to do with bed-wetting, and I had played a junior high school English teacher who had been sympathetic to the young boy with the problem. Wilson remembered me from the film, but I had the feeling he would have known me anyway. Canny and tough, Stuart Wilson knew just about everything that went on in the industry, and certainly all that transpired at Triangle, whether or not it was within his sphere of responsibility. He was older than most of the other network executives in town, somewhere in his early fifties, and he never lost an opportunity to take his younger colleagues down a peg or two. He was something of a dinosaur, having broken in at NBC during the Pat Weaver years, and had been with all four networks and several movie studios during his career. Steven Brandon had brought him to Triangle for the same reason football teams hire aging, past-their-prime quarterbacks: to give a sense of maturity and leadership to a group of less experienced up-and-comers. He had the raspy basso of a heavy smoker and a network of purplish veins on his nose attested to his fondness for spirits.

I asked him a lot of the same questions I'd put to Pritkin

and Schuyler and got a lot of the same answers, except that he seemed impatient to be rid of me and rather abrupt in his responses. I decided to try a more personal tack.

"You and Steven Brandon socialize sometimes, don't you?" I asked.

"I don't know what you mean by that," he said. "He's a bachelor and I'm a married grandfather-soon-to-be, so we don't hang out after hours that much. We have lunch usually once or twice a week, and we often wind up at the same parties. If that's socializing, I plead guilty."

"I don't think it's a question of guilt or innocence, Mr. Wilson."

"I gather you have some silly-ass notion that the bomb was meant for Steven instead of that kid."

"I'm not ruling it out, let's put it that way."

"And you're trying to figure out if one of us here at the network did it?"

"I'm not ruling that out, either."

"Do the police know you're doing this shit?"

"They haven't asked, and I haven't told them."

"Suppose I told them? Suppose I called whoever is in charge of that investigation and told them a private detective was hassling me?"

"If you said that, you'd be lying. I'm not hassling you. Mr. Brandon arranged this interview; it wasn't my idea, and whatever the police would say about it would be between them and me."

He coughed a hacking smoker's cough and leaned back in his chair. His shirt sleeves were rolled up to reveal muscular, hairy arms. "Well, fuck it, I don't give a damn that you're here. I don't like to be made to feel like a laboratory specimen, that's all."

"Overreacting a bit, aren't you?"

"Maybe I am. But let me enlighten you on a point or two

here. If I were an executive in the automobile business, or the oil business, or the steel business, or the pharmaceutical business, I'd be just hitting my stride. Around here I'm a fossil. I'm the only guy within miles of here who remembers Ernie Kovacs or saw 'I Love Lucy' when it was first-run. People look at me like I survived the Spanish-American War. So I have to be twice as good, run twice as fast, move twice as cute as any of these little shits with their blow-dried hairdos and designer sunglasses. I don't like it when people come around and start poking at me and rocking the boat. I'm hanging on here by my goddamn fingernails, you understand?"

"Anything you say stays with me, Mr. Wilson, unless it has a bearing on who killed Robbie Bingham. How's that?"

He waved a nicotine-stained hand in front of his face, all at once weary of the fight, and made a noise halfway between a sigh and a wheeze.

"Since we're talking off the record," I said, "what's your personal opinion of Steven Brandon?"

"He's one of the few guys in this town with the sense to hire someone like me. Most of the little shits don't want me around because I'll know it when they fuck up, and they don't have the brains to realize that maybe my experience could keep them from doing it."

"Is that an affirmative vote, then?"

He shrugged his broad shoulders. "There's good and there's bad in everybody," he said. "That's some of Brandon's good. The rest is that he's smart as a whip, he's got balls the size of watermelons, and he won't let anyone fuck him over. He knows when he's right and he fights for it."

"And the bad?"

"What?"

"There's good and bad in everyone, you said. What's Brandon's bad?"

"Off the record?"

"I said so."

He cogitated for a long moment, in the manner of one deciding how to bet the daily double. Then he said, "I'd have to be nuts to sit here and run down Steven Brandon when he's the one hiring you."

"I've told you I won't repeat anything you say to him."

"Well, screw it. Steven Brandon is the original Sammy Glick: he's ambitious, he's a publicity hog and a credit grabber, and he's a brain-picker."

"In what way?"

"I get a little tired of hearing 'boy genius' all the time. Everything that he's put on the air has come from one of us here on the row—Sanda Schuyler, Irv Pritkin, myself. There isn't an ounce of creativity in Steven Brandon's sawed-off little body. That's okay; he's a decision maker and he doesn't have to be creative. But he picks our brains and then takes all the bows. And he does it right in front of our faces."

"You all resent that?"

"Ah, shit. I've got a nice house in Studio City, I drive a nice car, I get all the perks, and I've got no complaints. If I'd wanted to be a celebrity I would have become an actor, like you."

"I'm hardly a celebrity."

"That's because you're too busy running around being Sam Spade to pay attention to your acting career. By the way, you did a nice job for us in *Calico Cat*. I meant to tell you that when you came in."

"Thanks," I said. "Acting seems a little bit unimportant when you get involved in life-or-death situations like this."

"If I saw that line in a script I'd blue-pencil it. Awfully melodramatic."

"Mr. Wilson, someone has already died. It could have been Steven Brandon."

"You're looking for a Mad Bomber here, Saxon, and that's

the long and short of it. Bothering Steven's friends is not only a waste of time, it's goddamn insulting."

"I'm sorry your skin is so thin, Mr. Wilson."

"Me? Shit, I'm the original rhino-hide. In this business you have to be."

"Good. Then you won't mind telling me where you were on the morning Steven Brandon was injured."

"I mind like hell."

"Why?"

"Because my reputation in this business is spotless. I never took a nickel in thirty years, not from anybody. I paid for my own lunches, my own vacations, and if you look around you'll notice there's no casting couch in this office. I resent the implication."

His rather substantial ears had reddened during his peroration, and he coughed at the end of it. I just waited, looking at him, staring him down, until finally he looked away from me, stubbed out his cigarette in an already overflowing ashtray, and lit another one. Then he met my eyes again.

"You're pretty tough yourself, aren't you?"

"How's that?"

"You know I could put in a bad word for you in the casting department at this network, don't you?"

"I suppose so. But I don't care for threats, Mr. Wilson. There are other networks. And even if there weren't, I think I'd rather shovel horse manure than knuckle under to crap like that."

"You also know I could break you in half. I used to be a major in the marines."

I sighed. "That's used to be. I've got fifteen years on you. If you want to take a swing, that's your option. I don't think you will, though."

"Why not?"

"A couple of reasons. First of all, you're too insecure about your job. You talk rough and ready, but as you said earlier, you've got to be better than the little shits. Conservative TV networks take a dim view of their vice presidents throwing punches. Especially since your boss asked you to talk to me."

He was very quiet, peering at me through the smoke. "You said a couple of reasons."

"Let it pass," I said.

"I don't think I will."

"Okay, the second reason is you really don't think you can finish it. Am I right or wrong?"

The air seemed to go out of him; he looked older. The strain of keeping one step ahead of the younger executives nipping at his heels was beginning to leave him short of breath. He said, "You're right, damn it. I'm sorry. I'm pretty hard-nosed sometimes. To survive as long as I have you've got to be."

"Then I suppose you will answer my question?"

"What question is that?"

"Where were you on the morning of the thirteenth when that bomb went off on Cicada Drive?"

He put his hand up to his mouth, wiping the corners of it with his thumb and forefinger. He said, "I was in my car on the way to work like I always am in the mornings. My wife was still asleep when I left—she's not well, she sleeps late mornings—so I can't prove it. Are you going to call the cops on me?"

"Not yet," I said.

Back at the office Jo was waiting for me to get in before she went to lunch. There were several telephone messages on the spike on her desk, but she pulled them away from me when I reached for them.

"First things first," she said. "I had a long talk with a Father

Beemer," she said. "He operates a halfway house for runaways in Hollywood."

"I'm not sure you'd classify Marvel as a runaway," I said.

"Maybe not, but he sure isn't living with his folks, so he qualifies. Anyway, Father Beemer wants to talk to you. He thinks he might be able to place Marvel somewhere and get him into a school."

"Great!" I said.

"In the meantime, are you going to keep him with you?"

"Unless you'd like to take him," I said.

"My marriage is under enough strain just with me working for you," she said. "I don't need more."

"Who else called?"

"They'll keep. Talk to Father Beemer."

She handed me a slip of paper with his number, and I went inside and made an appointment to see him later that afternoon. He sounded harried. As soon as I hung up, Jo came in with the other messages.

"I'm impressed," she said. "A call from a Hollywood immortal and a network head all on the same morning. Makes Jennifer London seem unimportant, whoever she may be." She crooked a quizzical eyebrow at me. "I'd say from my instinct that she's auditioning for Bimbo of the Month."

"Why do you assume every woman that comes near me is a bimbo?"

"Because it usually turns out that way. If you'd only find a nice girl and settle down—"

"Every time I find a nice girl you call her a bimbo."

"It's a vicious cycle," she said, and went back out to her desk in the outer office. Sometimes Jo's Jiminy Cricket act wears thin.

I called my client, who didn't seem to be in a terrific mood.

"I hear you've been bouncing my staff around," he said.

"I wouldn't call it that."

"I want a report."

"I don't have what you might call results, Mr. Brandon, if you mean did I find out who was trying to kill you."

He didn't say anything for a while, but I could hear impatience in his breathing pattern. Then he said, "What did you find out?"

"Everyone thinks you're a saint."

"They're lying."

"They couldn't *all* be lying."

"If they said they loved me, they are. It eats away at Sanda Schuyler that she'll never be number one at this network because she happens to sit down to pee, and I'm sure she thinks I'm a male chauvinist pig who's trying to block her advancement. Irv Pritkin is scared shitless about his job, and the one he's most scared of is yours truly. Stu Wilson thinks I steal all the credit at the network, and he's right. And I understand you went to see Raina."

"I did."

"That's none of your goddamn business, you know."

"Everything is my business, Mr. Brandon," I said, "as long as you're paying me to do a job." I took a deep breath. "If you want to terminate that arrangement, just say the word."

"Don't get testy with me. I want you to stay away from Raina because what we have is what we have, with no illusions. Besides, I know she didn't do it because she was in the shower when I left. Beyond the sex and the booze we hardly know each other. So that's that."

"Not necessarily," I said. "I have some more checking to do."

"Well, what's your impression so far? And I mean the bottom line."

"The bottom line? Most people consider you a highly talented and extremely valuable son of a bitch."

He laughed, to my relief. "Very observant of you," he said, "but you're not telling me anything I don't know."

"I'm working on it," I said. "How are you feeling?"

"How do you think I'm feeling? Like dog crap."

"That's good," I said. "I'll check back with you later."

I hung up and called Raina Stone.

"Just wanted to tell you what a great kisser you are," she said, "and to let you know you can come back anytime."

"That's very nice of you—Raina." I'd almost made the mistake of calling her Miss Stone again. And once you've kissed like she and I had kissed it's kind of silly to stand on formality.

"How about tonight?" she said.

"I'm afraid I'm pretty busy working on the case," I told her.

"Scared of Steven finding out?"

"Let's just say it would complicate my job."

I could hear her lighting a cigarette. She'd probably been drinking slowly but steadily the whole morning. "Don't feel bad," she said, "the whole world's afraid of Steven. Join the club." She waited a moment, then said, "Well, pal, it's your loss. See you in the funny papers."

As I hung up I reflected on how long it had been since I'd heard that expression. Maybe Raina Stone was still living in the past, along with Stu Wilson and his memories of Ernie Kovacs. Along with me, who won't listen to any music written after 1968. Along with more than half of the rest of the country who regularly get ignored by the media tastemakers.

Jennifer London answered her phone on the first ring. "What a pleasant surprise to get your message, Jennifer," I said. "Really gave a lift to my day."

"Well," she said, and her voice was tinkly like Japanese wind chimes, "I just got to thinking about you, that you were really nice, and I was wondering if the dinner invitation was still open."

"Indeed it is," I said. If I couldn't seem to get a break in this damn case, perhaps things were turning a corner for me socially. Jennifer London was definitely a candle in the darkness, at least in looks. Whether or not she would prove to be anything more than a pretty face and body remained to be seen. "What night did you have in mind?"

"Tonight?" she said, with a little upturned inflection of hope. "I know it's short notice, but I suddenly became free and—I hope you're not feeling like you're second choice or anything."

"Even if I am, I'd be delighted to see you tonight." I picked up a pencil. "Where do you live?"

She gave me an address in Brentwood, not too far from my own place in the Palisades, and told me she'd be ready at about eight o'clock. Considering my late afternoon appointment with Father Beemer, that would probably work out just fine. And then she said, "What are you wearing?"

"Basic black with pearls," I said. It was an ineffectual attempt to amuse, and not only did it not work but there was a sharp intake of breath on the other end of the line, and then in a voice not nearly so musical, she said, "What's that supposed to mean?"

"Just kidding," I said. It seemed that whatever Jennifer's attributes might be, a quick sense of humor was not one of them. "I'll probably wear a sports jacket with an open shirt. Is that okay?"

"Oh," she said. "Okay. Sure. See you at eight."

I was getting a bit hungry, but since I was planning on a big dinner with Jennifer that evening I decided to skip lunch and have a granola bar from my desk drawer instead. I pride myself on being a gourmet—"foodie" is really more like it, if the truth be known—but I make no apology for eating granola bars for lunch. They are a thousandfold better than any of the fast-food nightmares available in the vicinity of my office. And washed down with a cup of good coffee they aren't half bad.

I was just finishing up the aforementioned coffee when Jo buzzed me on the intercom and told me that Barry Haworth was in the outer office. My day was full of surprises, it seemed.

"I hope you don't mind my dropping by like this," he said when Jo had ushered him in. His bulk made me fear for the future of the chair into which he sank.

"Not at all," I said, "although I'm a bit surprised. What can I do for you?"

"It's what I can do for you," he said.

I waited, expectantly.

"The word is all over the street this morning that you beat the hell out of Tony Haselhorst."

"Tony Hasel—oh. Ugly, pasty-faced guy, dirty-blond hair, runs boys on Santa Monica Boulevard?"

Barry nodded.

"I don't remember leaving him a résumé. How does the word get out?"

Barry shrugged, which is roughly equivalent to an avalanche on Pike's Peak. "Jungle drums," he said. "There's a grapevine in Boys Town, just like anywhere else. And the word is that a good-looking guy with gray hair and a blue Fiat convertible smashed Haselhorst's face up pretty bad and stole his number-one boy. The description seems to fit you. So does the bad temper."

"Forget the temper part, will you?"

"An elephant never forgets," he said with a little smile of self-mockery. "Do you have Marvel?"

"I'm not even going to answer that, Barry. I really appreciate your coming here, but you'd be best served by knowing as little as possible."

He crossed his large ankles almost delicately. "Haselhorst

doesn't know who you are. Only a few of us do—me, for instance. And Jimmy, who's one of Haselhorst's boys. Jimmy'll tell if Haselhorst asks him, but as far as I know it hasn't occurred to him that Jimmy would know."

"And you?"

He looked down for a moment, and the facial skin that wasn't covered by hair flushed red. "Haselhorst and I just . . . do business together sometimes," he said. "I don't owe him a damn thing." Then he looked up and fluttered his eyelashes at me. "I'd really stay out of Boys Town if I were you," he said, "because if Haselhorst ever does find out who you are, he's going to kill you."

○ 10 ○

The house was squat and wide, like a big-league catcher hunkering down behind the plate; dirty white with greenish trim, it hadn't been painted in a long time. There were hanging planters on the porch, but whatever plants had once inhabited them were long dead, victims of neglect like the neighborhood itself, a block off La Brea Avenue in Hollywood in the northernmost reaches of Boys Town. The sign that hung from the eaves should have been advertising a chiropractic clinic or a thrift shop, but it read SAINT STEPHEN'S MISSION, and it creaked as it swung in the wind, a ghost-town relic in the middle of a huge, bustling city. I climbed the cement steps and took the sign on the other side of the glass door that read ENTER at its word.

In the entry hall was an inexpensive plaster statue of the saint who had given his name to the mission, Saint Stephen the Martyr, whose lot it had been to perish in a fusillade of stones while young Saul of Tarsus looked on, and whose expression, at least on this particular statue, seemed typical of the type of martyrdom more often associated with Jewish mothers. I personally think the saint for whom my Chicago alma mater was named, Saint Aloysius, who had died without ever in his life having committed a mortal sin, was even more of a martyr. As the Saint Al's boys used to say when taunting hunting packs of teens from some other parish, Saint Stephen wasn't shit compared to Saint Aloysius.

The house smelled musty and gray, as if someone very old had lived there for more than fifty years and then died quietly in his sleep one morning, a decade's worth of neatly and chronologically arranged copies of the *Los Angeles Times* unread. It was the kind of mustiness no amount of airing-out could dispel, going clear through the plastered walls to the beams and joists and foundation. The house seemed to be dying of old age.

I wasn't sure whether I was in a holy place or a flophouse, so I called out my "Hello?" rather tentatively, not wanting to waste any reverence where it wasn't needed but hating to take any chances. I heard some vague stirrings from the back of the house, and then a short slight figure dressed in black appeared at the end of the hallway. He peered myopically through the gloom, then started down the corridor toward me. He wasn't wearing his jacket, and the sleeves of his black shirt were rolled up to the elbow, displaying thin, untanned arms. His stiff ecclesiastical collar dug into the flesh under his jaw, making me wonder why all priests didn't have a severe skin rash on their neck.

"You must be Mr. Saxon," he said in a high, almost lyrical voice, and extended his hand. "I'm Father Beemer."

He was dark-haired and the soft, light brown eyes seemed almost out of place in his face. He had no chin to speak of, and what was there was pulled in so that it nearly disappeared into his collar, for which he tried to compensate by thrusting his head forward, giving him the appearance of a man forever waiting for someone to drop a piano on him. His handshake was soft, almost apologetic, and he guided me back along the stale-smelling corridor to what evidently was once the master bedroom but now served as a mean office. He handed me into an uncomfortable straight-backed chair with arms and went around to sit behind his desk, which wasn't much of a desk at all but seemed to be an old dinette table that had, like so many other Catholics, been converted. There was a picture of Jesus on the wall, an agonized, suffering Jesus on the cross, and at right angles to it on another wall was a wooden crucifix on which Christ seemed to be at rest. Apparently martyrdom in its many forms was the order of the day at Saint Stephen's. The old memories stirred in me, the ones Saint Al had put there that would never completely disappear, and I wondered if Father Beemer was going to rap my knuckles.

"The lady I spoke to this morning—Mrs. Zeidler, was it?—said we have a runaway?"

"I don't know exactly who or what he is, Father," I said. "I know he was working as a prostitute down the street a bit and was in the process of getting a beating from his pimp when I came by and decided he was better off somewhere else. I haven't been able to get much out of him. He may have a learning disability."

The priest made a cathedral out of his fingertips and pursed his lips. I'm not sure if all priests have done that since the Church was founded or whether it simply postdates Barry Fitzgerald in *Going My Way*. In any event, Father Beemer sat like that for a time, then looked up at me.

"Please don't be offended, Mr. Saxon, but what exactly is your involvement with this boy?"

"I'm not offended and I have no involvement. I'm a private investigator and I spoke to Marvel about another matter. When I saw him on the street I recognized him and stepped in to do my knight-in-shining-armor number, that's all."

"I see," Beemer said. "This other matter—it wouldn't have something to do with that car-bombing a few weeks ago?"

Father Beemer had the annoying habit of ending every sentence with a question mark.

"Yes it would, Father, as a matter of fact. Marvel was pointed out to me in the first place as being the best friend of the boy—the young man—who was killed."

"And that is your only interest in him?"

"Why don't you say what you mean, Father?"

"I think you know what I mean."

"I've told you my interest isn't anything personal. I dislike seeing children abused, whether they're in preschool, on the dean's list, or selling it on the street." I tried to relax in the wooden chair, one of the famous Torquemada line of fine rectory furniture so prized by the Church. "You know about the bombing, Father?"

"I read the papers," he said, "and I know a lot of the boys on the street. Many of them come through here, you know."

"Did you know Robbie Bingham?"

"I knew of him. We usually deal with younger boys here."

"Boys only?"

He shrugged. "This is West Hollywood, Mr. Saxon."

"So what is the word on the street, about the bombing?"

Father Beemer shuffled some papers on the dinette table. "Anytime a homosexual is killed it causes a certain amount of concern within the gay community. What with the current AIDS scare, homophobia can run high sometimes. I've had at least three boys come off the street voluntarily since the bombing."

"And what do you do with them?"

"Keep them until we can get them placed in foster homes within the archdiocese. Good homes, understanding homes."

"You don't try to get them back to their parents?"

"Sometimes we do. But usually when they show up here they're just about out of options."

"I see. About Marvel, Father. I think he's around fifteen, he's black, and a little—slow. And as far as I can tell, he's all alone. That sounds like a tough placement."

He raised both hands in a gesture of resignation. Despite his swarthy complexion he very much resembled the statue of Saint Stephen the Martyr. "Why don't you keep Marvel with you?"

"That's out of the question," I said. "I'm a bachelor, I'm heterosexual, I have an erratic profession—two erratic professions. I wouldn't know what to do with him."

"So," he said, "your charity lets you save a boy from a beating but doesn't go any farther?"

"I thought Jewish people were the guilt-layers, Father. You're giving Catholicism a whole new dimension here. I'm sorry, but you can't work that kind of magic on me. I like the boy and I want what's good for him, and I'm ready and willing to make substantial contributions, within my means, to help him get started. I'll maintain an interest, talk to the kid once in a while, spend some time with him, take him to the ball game—" I stopped. I realized I was babbling. Father Beemer looked fairly pleased with himself. I took a big gulp of air and said, "I'm sure you realize why that isn't possible."

Beemer stood up, his shoulders just a bit lower than when I'd first come in. "I had to take my shot," he said. "When can you have the boy here?"

"Tomorrow, first thing in the morning."

"I'll have a bed ready for him. After I've talked to him I'll start making some inquiries. Mr. Saxon, I didn't mean to put you on the spot. You've been very kind to this boy."

"I know it's a spit in the ocean."

He nodded. "There are more than a hundred of them on Santa Monica Boulevard alone," he said. "Even if I had the room here I couldn't begin to find good homes for them. But one does what one can."

We walked together down the long corridor toward the front door and I remembered Jimmy Cagney and Pat O'Brien, hoodlum and priest, walking more than one last mile together. When we reached the statue of the Martyr and Beemer put his hand on the door to see me out, I said, "Marvel aside, Father, if the jungle telegraph puts anything out about that bombing, I'd appreciate it if you'd give me a call."

He let his hand fall from the doorknob. "I don't know about the bombing," he said. "But I know there was someone Robbie was having a lot of trouble with—that he was frightened of."

I took out my notebook and a brown felt pen. "Then that's the guy I want to talk to."

"He's not very pleasant to talk to at the best of times," Father Beemer said, "but you can try. His name is Tony Haselhorst."

First things first. The two divergent roads down which this case was taking me were beginning to make my head ache. I needed the evening off. In any event, Tony Haselhorst was best approached in the morning. Most pimps were night people; mornings did not find them at their best. Nor me, for that matter, but at least I would have surprise on my side. Tonight was for relaxation.

I explained to Marvel about Father Beemer's and that he'd be there for a while until they could put him into a foster home, and he looked fairly skeptical. When I told him he'd be attending a school he was downright cynical.

"I dumb," he said. "Ain't no school gonna let me in, fool." He didn't pronounce the final *l*. "They don' want no dummies."

I sat down next to him on the sofa, and with the remote-control switch I flicked off the television, the first time it had been silent since he'd arrived the night before.

"You're not dumb, Marvel, quit talking about yourself like that. You've got some catching up to do, but you're not dumb. Say that."

"Shit," he said.

"Say it or I'm taking the TV control with me tonight."

He shook his head, humoring me. "I ain' dumb," he said.

"Say it again and mean it."

"Not for real?"

"Say it!"

"I ain' dumb," he said.

"Now, anytime anyone tells you you are, you tell them you're not. And more important, tell yourself. Understand?"

"Sho," he said. "I ain' dumb."

I'd stopped at the market and gotten a slab of great-looking spareribs. I went into the kitchen and whipped up my own special brand of barbecue sauce, made with ground peanuts and New Mexican *chipotle* peppers, slathered it generously all over the ribs, and put them in the oven to bake. Then I fixed a green salad with cucumber and tomatoes and jicama and made a simple oil-and-vinegar dressing with rosemary and put it in the refrigerator for when Marvel was ready for dinner. I washed a russet Idaho and put it in the microwave and set it for six minutes so that all Marvel would have to do was push the Start button, and then I went in to get ready for my date. Marvel came and sat on the edge of what had become his bed and chatted with me about the kind of place Beemer ran and even a bit about the prospect of his soon-to-be school, and then he said, "Is they bitches?" and I asked him to repeat it, and the third time I figured out that he was asking if there would be girls at school.

"Girls?" I said.

He nodded almost shyly. "I only do that other stuff because Tony say."

I sat down on the bed next to him, one sock on and the other in my hand. I was having trouble assimilating that little piece of information. "Marvel," I said, "you're just full of surprises."

Jennifer London lived in a sprawling apartment complex near Sunset Boulevard in fashionable Brentwood. It was the kind of place that was known, in the seventies, as a "singles complex," equipped as it was with pools, tennis courts, saunas, Jacuzzis, exercise rooms, and an enormous common room in which Sunday brunch was served. It was normally thought of as a halfway house for the newly divorced, since most of the apartments were furnished with high-style inexpensive furniture. There was a forced gaiety about the place; the assistant manager was known as a "social director."

Jennifer looked only sensational, even though she hadn't quite finished putting on her makeup, in a vivid blue jersey dress that seemed to cling to her in all the places it was supposed to. With most women, makeup is essential to the illusion; with Jennifer it was merely gilding the lily.

"Oh, God, I'm sorry, I'm running late," she said when she opened the door. "I'm a mess and the place is a mess. Come on in and sit down; I won't be a minute." This was all spoken in such a breathless rush I couldn't have responded to it if I'd wanted to. She fled into her bedroom and I sat down on the sofa. The morning's *Los Angeles Times* was tossed haphazardly on one end of it and the cushions on the other end were mashed down. Cigarette butts with dark-brown lipstick stains overflowed the ashtray on the coffee table and the whole place smelled of stale cigarette smoke. Elevator music came softly from an expensive stereo against the wall..

"Fix yourself a drink," she said from the open doorway. "Everything you need is on the bar."

"Do you want one, too?"

"Whatever you're having," she said, "as long as it isn't bourbon. In fact, I don't think I have any bourbon."

"One anything-but-bourbon coming up," I said. The bar was really more of a room divider between the living room and the efficiency kitchen, but it was fairly well stocked with bottles—decanters, actually, with little engraved labels hanging around their necks from delicate gold chains. I chose the one that said SCOTCH and built two on the rocks, then put just a splash of water in hers. I took a sip: Black Label, it tasted like.

"Here's your drink," I called. "Shall I bring it in? You need me to hook or button or zip anything?"

"Your lip," she called out, and then she came out of the

bedroom looking even more radiant than the first time I'd seen her at Mayan Auto Rentals. She indicated the drinks.

"Are you going to drink both of those?"

I handed her the one with water and we clinked glasses. I sat back down on the sofa and she put her drink down, gathered up the newspapers, dumped the stained butts into the middle of the sports section, and disappeared into the kitchen area for a moment. She came back without the trash and sat down on the far end of the sofa.

"Did you have much trouble finding the place?"

"It sits up on a hill with two hundred and eighty apartments and two lighted tennis courts. The palace at Versailles would be harder to find."

"I meant once you got into the complex."

"No, your directions were impeccable. As is your outfit. You're quite a stunner, young lady."

"Thanks, but it hasn't gotten me anyplace so far."

"You're an actress?"

"Aspiring. *Per*-spiring—and sometimes I think *ex*-piring."

"I do a little acting myself," I said. "It can be a pretty rough business."

"You don't know the half of it."

"I don't?"

"No," she said. "You're a man."

"I can't see where that would make a difference."

"That's because you don't have ugly little gnomes crawling all over you grabbing your tits just because they happen to have the power to hire you."

"This is a sexy business. I never heard of anyone having to screw the boss to get a job at an insurance company."

"It happens."

"I'm sure it does."

"I'm at the point where every time I see a movie I wonder who the female star had to put out for. All men think with their dicks."

"I know you're bitter," I said, "but I don't personally know of any producer or director who would jeopardize his picture for a free piece. They work too hard to get where they are. There are some minor-leaguers who do that sort of thing, but that's why they're minor-leaguers and likely to stay that way. Most of the people in movies and TV are there because they love it; they enjoy the work."

"I can relate to that," she said. "I love acting. Studied in New York to learn my craft."

"You'll probably make it, then. Just hang in there and try to ignore the bullshit."

"That's like going swimming in the swamp and trying to ignore the alligators." She belted down most of her drink. "Are you going to feed me?"

"I'm going to feed you to the alligators," I said.

It's not much of a drive from Brentwood to the ocean, unless you take the twists and turns of Sunset Boulevard, in which case it's a test of your reflexes, responses, and hand-eye coordination. It's also very romantic, and though it's just moments from some of the most heavily populated areas of western Los Angeles, you get the feeling of being out in the country. That's the route I chose to get to my favorite little seafood restaurant halfway between Santa Monica and the overpriced status-conscious watering holes of Malibu. It was decided on the drive that Jennifer was more interested in good food than ambience, and food being somewhat of a passion with me, I just happened to know a place. We didn't talk about much of anything in the car except to comment on some of the more pretentious homes along Sunset and to exclaim over the occasional spectacular glimpses of the sun saying its pinkish-orange good night to the ocean, visible on the curves that obviously had given the boulevard its name.

By the time we got to the restaurant and waited for a window table, there wasn't much left to look at except the surf lit up by the restaurant's glow. We ordered a dusty-dry Chardonnay and decided to look at each other.

"So tell me," she said after we had toasted each other and critiqued the wine, "how's it going on your case? Any hot suspects?"

I laughed. "Jennifer, you're seeing too many movies. I'm just doing a routine investigation and poking around asking questions. That's all."

"It must be fascinating, doing what you do. And dangerous. I'll bet you're really brave."

Jennifer had an invaluable talent, one that had undoubtedly been given to most of the world's great courtesans: the ability to make a man feel he is without exception the most enthralling human being she's ever met. I am not unsusceptible to charms like that, and I found myself recounting the details of some of my past cases like some windy old bore at a London gentleman's club. Her gaze never wavered from my face. The fact that more than ninety percent of a private investigator's time is spent tracing skips for loan companies, investigating insurance claims, and spying on errant husbands or wives or sticky-fingered business partners didn't slow me down a bit.

"Take this bombing thing," Jennifer said as I refilled her glass. "I mean, where would you start? How would you know who to talk to and what questions to ask?"

"Most of it's common sense. It's like a jigsaw puzzle: you look for the missing piece."

Her eyes were bottomless. "I'll bet you don't miss many pieces, do you?" And then she was not quite so provocative as she said, "What's your missing piece here?"

"Where?"

"The car-bombing, silly."

"Jennifer, I don't like to talk about—"

"It's not like I'm a stranger. My God, I *am* a part of this whole thing. I mean, I rented the killer the death car."

"Hot suspects, death cars," I said. "You sound like the front page of the *New York Post*."

"Oh, you know what I mean."

"Yes, I know what you mean. I'd just rather not talk about it until it's over."

"When will that be? I mean, are you close?"

"When did you become Nancy Drew?"

"I'm kind of involved, for one thing. And you know, after you gave me your card at the rental place, I just got to thinking about it. I've never met a private eye before."

"Please, no more clichés. Next you'll be calling me a gumshoe."

"Well, whatever. I just thought you were a very interesting, even fascinating man. And you're very good-looking. So I wanted to get to know you."

"That's very flattering," I said, "but private investigators are just like everyone else. Prick us, do we not bleed?"

"I think you're being modest. I think you have this case all wrapped up tight and you're just not telling me about it. It's part of your, what, your mystique?"

"A bigger part of my mystique," I said as the waiter arrived, "is my excellent sense of food. So if you'll permit me, I'm going to order for both of us."

She leaned back in her chair. "I'm in your hands," she said.

"It's a beginning," I said.

We began with baby shrimp, smoked and served with a cream and dill sauce with feta cheese, and a plate of green-lipped mussels in a garlic sauce that you just had to sop up with your roll. I ordered a poached Norwegian salmon and a simple but elegant shark piccata, and Jennifer and I split everything so we wouldn't miss out on something tasty. We also put away another bottle of the Chardonnay, and for dessert some white chocolate ice cream and an almond cheesecake that was almost too sweet. My dinner companion had a healthy appetite, and we laughed and talked about memorable dinners we'd had in the past. I bragged a bit of a few that I had cooked, and for a while over coffee we just held hands and watched the waves crash on the rocks below, the drops of foam giving off their own luminescence in the muted glow.

When we had consumed just about all the coffee that was reasonably good for us, I leaned over and said, "Would you like to go somewhere and listen to music? Or dance?"

"Slow dancing," she said. "I think I'd like to be in your arms."

There are precious few places in Los Angeles where one can dance the way they used to, with a man holding the woman by the hand and about the waist, but there was one kind of archaic place in Santa Monica that often served in a pinch if one were not too fussy. The band consisted of a middle-aged lady playing piano and organ, a thirty-five-ish man playing guitar, and a drummer who looked like a marine boot on his first liberty. As the hostess explained to us as she showed us to a booth, "They quit at twelve. That's because they start at seven-thirty and play for the dinner crowd—you know, soft, easy-listening stuff. After nine, though, they get a little crazy."

I looked at the organist, her hair in a forties bun, peering at her sheet music through horn-rimmed glasses, and was glad we'd gotten there after nine to see her get a little crazy. We ordered drinks from the hostess, not even bothering to sit down first, and moved out on the floor to the strains of "To All the Girls I've Loved Before," which the lady, who also sang, changed to "All the Men," and stayed there for one of the more curious renditions of "In the Mood" I've come across. Jennifer was a somewhat awkward dancer, strange for a woman who walked with such grace and poise, but her body did feel good against mine, and she made sure that I felt every curve and mound and soft place, her head laid on my shoulder as though she were asleep but the pressure of her thighs and breasts and hips against me assuring me that she was not sleeping at all.

Her bed was a queen-size water bed with a mirror in the headboard. I undressed her slowly, especially since she wasn't wearing that much to begin with. The dress coming off over her head made her hair look that much more deliciously rumpled. She wore no bra, and her breasts were perfect, red-tipped and creamy soft. She wore very sheer pantyhose, and beneath them a pair of light blue panties that would have complemented the dress had anyone been able to see them while she was wearing the dress. I try to be a slow love-maker, mainly because it's the best thing to do in the whole world and I can't see any reason for rushing it. But Jennifer was aggressive, her arm snaking around my neck to pull my head down to where she could almost devour my mouth with hers. She writhed whenever I touched naked flesh, and I did that a lot. Her fingers dug into the back of my shoulders and she moaned as her tongue lashed in and out of my mouth.

And then I ran my hand down across her hip, over the fleecy mound and between her legs, and she stiffened. My fingers were gentle and probing, but she was bone dry. I could sense something was very wrong, from the way her breathing had changed and from the dryness between her labia, and I moved up and away from her a bit and looked at her with what I hoped was coming off like concern.

She sighed. "Sorry," she said. "Guess maybe I've had too much to drink."

"That's okay," I said. Rather lamely, I thought later.

"Maybe it was just too soon."

"Hey. It happens, you know?"

Jennifer said, "In the best of families."

"Right."

I rolled away from her and we just lay there for a bit. I said, "I don't suppose you have a cigarette around anywhere?"

She shook her head. I wasn't looking at her but I heard the rustle of the pillowcase. "I don't smoke," she said.

"That's okay."

"Look, I'm really sorry."

I moved over on my side so I was facing her. "It's really all right," I said. "No harm done."

"It's just—"

Uh-oh. Two of the most frightening words in the language when used in tandem that way: *It's just—*

"What?"

She shrugged and pulled the overhang of the bedspread up around her to cover her nudity. "I don't know, I guess I'm really uptight about this murder business."

"No reason why you should be."

"I can identify him. The killer. He must know that. What if he comes after me? I'm scared—really scared."

I stuck my arm under her head, feeling the luxurious softness of her hair in the crook of my arm, and gently pulled her into a cuddling position. I love to cuddle, and tonight it seemed I was settling for my second choice. "Nobody's going to come after you, Jen. He probably looks different than when he rented the car anyway, and he'll probably figure you rent so many cars to so many people that you won't even remember him."

"Even so, I've been just terrified."

Jennifer didn't seem like the kind of woman who got terrified. I said, "They're going to get him. Don't worry."

"Maybe," she said, snuggling closer and licking my neck, "if you told me who you suspected I'd know who to watch out for."

"I suspect everyone, Jennifer," I said. "I even suspect you a little bit."

She stayed lying on my arm but moved away from me. "It didn't seem to affect your zipper," she said in a voice that was several degrees below zero.

"I didn't mean it that way. I suspect everyone, because that way I don't get any surprises. I hate surprises."

"I certainly didn't expect to wind up in bed with a man who thought I was a killer."

"Jennifer—" I sighed. I had experience with this type of person: unreasonable, bullheaded, and ready to pounce on whatever one might say and turn it into a negative. "It's just something to say. I don't suspect you, okay?"

"Then who do you suspect?"

I took my arm out from under her head.

"Can't you see how scared I am?"

"Yes, but I can't help you. If I had any answers I'd go to the police with them."

She threw her left arm over her eyes as if to protect them from the glare, even though the only light was a pink-shaded bulb clear across the room. "I don't know," she said. "It's all going wrong. I guess you'd better go."

"Was it something I did?" I said.

"No. I'm just not used to falling into bed with every man who takes me to dinner, and I just got scared all of a sudden. It's not you, sweetheart."

But her tone told me that it was.

I got dressed quickly. She made no attempt to move but just lay on top of the covers with a corner of the spread thrown over her. She didn't say anything else until I told her I'd call her.

"You don't want to call me," she said. "I'm just a frigid bitch."

"There's no such thing. Hey, come on, Jennifer, I'm not angry or anything. It's not such a big deal. We'll both live."

She looked up at me and smiled dimly. "You've got a rain check, okay?"

I bent down and kissed her gently on the corner of her mouth. "Sure it's okay," I told her.

That's what I told her. But I drove home with one of the most painful cases of blue balls I'd experienced since I was sixteen years old and going home from an above-the-waist-only necking session with Genevieve Mascari.

o 11 o

In the morning I packed up the few belongings Marvel owned. I had given him a toothbrush, a couple of sweatshirts and an old sweater, and I also packed a couple of disposable plastic razors I'd had around the apartment. He didn't say much. He'd watched his cartoons during the time I was showering and dressing, and had killed off an entire box of Special K and more than a quart of milk. He was a growing boy.

"Marvel," I said, "maybe on Saturday morning I can pick you up and we'll go shopping for some good clothes for you, okay?"

"Tha's cool," he said without much enthusiasm.

"Look," I said, "you're going to be fine. They'll get you to school, you'll learn how to read better, and then maybe they can find you a job. You'll stay with Father Beemer for a while and then they'll find a nice home for you to live in. Doesn't that sound great?"

Apparently it didn't, because there was no answer. I felt lousy, if you want to know the truth, but there didn't seem to be much I could do about it. The kid wasn't making it any easier for me. After a while he said, "They got TV at this father's place?"

"I don't know. I guess so. Everybody's got a TV."

"Not me," he said.

I knotted a tie around my neck. I don't know why I was even wearing one; I didn't usually. Then I went to the leather case in the bottom of my closet and took out the black leather shoulder holster with the .38 police special in it. I took the gun out and put it on the bed and started strapping on the leather. Marvel's eyes were two black-centered white saucers in his brown face.

"Shee-it," he said. "Can I see?"

I hesitated a moment, then checked to make sure the .38 wasn't loaded and handed it to him, butt first in the accepted fashion. He hefted it, sighted things around the room, and finally turned it on me.

"Never point a gun at anyone," I said, taking it from him, "unless you're planning to use it."

"It ain't loaded," he said.

"I don't care if it's a plastic squirt gun. I have a thing about guns pointed at me. Most people do." I took the cartridge box out of the case and loaded the chambers, then put an extra six rounds in the pocket of my jacket. I tucked the gun snugly beneath my left arm and buttoned my jacket.

"You gonna use that?"

"I hope not."

"Then why you carry it?"

"Just in case," I said.

Father Beemer greeted us in the entry hall. He didn't offer to shake hands with either of us. "So this is our newest customer," he said, hands in front of him briefly in an attitude of prayer. "What's your name, son?"

"Marvel," Marvel said.

"Marvel." He ran it around on his tongue as if tasting it for approval like a too-young but promising Zinfandel. "Well, Marvel, welcome to Saint Stephen's. I'm sure we'll get along. Do you know who Saint Stephen was, Marvel?"

Marvel shook his head.

"No, Father," Beemer prompted. "Saint Stephen was the first martyr. Do you know what a martyr is? A martyr is someone who suffers a great deal without complaining. Saint Stephen had to suffer for his faith, the way we all sometimes have to suffer."

I said, "Do you think we could postpone the catechism instruction until Marvel's seen where he's going to sleep?"

"Sorry," Beemer said. "Force of habit." And then he chuckled. "Old seminary joke—about nuns? Force of habit?"

"I got it," I said.

"Yes. Well, come this way."

Marvel and I followed the priest up the narrow creaking stairway and down the upstairs hall to the back of the house. There were two doors at the end of the corridor and Beemer opened the one on the right.

The room was as big as a large bathroom. There were two single cots and two small, cheap dressers with peeling paint. On the wall was an inexpensive framed lithograph of the Virgin Mary and another crucifix. Directly under the crucifix, sprawled on one of the cots, was a young man somewhere under twenty. He wore faded jeans and a black T-shirt, heavy biking boots, and at least three unmatched earrings in each ear. His head was shaved except for a three-inch ridge down the middle, and that stood up straight in four-inch-long spikes, pink, purple, and green in color, although there was so much gel on the hair it was hard to tell exactly what colors it was.

"Eddie," said Father Beemer, "I'd like you to meet Mr. Saxon and Marvel. Marvel's going to be your new roommate for a while."

The boy barely stirred from off his elbow. "Bull-*shit!*" he said with a rising inflection.

"Nice to meet you, too," I said.

"Gimme a break, Father," Eddie said. "I ain't gonna live with no boogie!"

"Now, Eddie," Father Beemer said, "we are all equal in the eyes of the Lord."

Marvel just looked at me.

"This will be your bed, Marvel," Father Beemer said. "You'll be responsible for making it every day, and for cleaning up after yourself in the bathroom. You're allowed to watch two hours of television each evening, and those privileges will be suspended if you don't keep things tidy around here. There's also a schedule of chores posted in the kitchen each week, and you'll be expected to do your share."

Marvel just looked at me.

"During the day, when you aren't in classes or taking religious instruction," Beemer said, "you're free to come and go. However, curfew is at eight o'clock in the evening. At nine o'clock we lock the doors to your rooms, and we unlock them at seven A.M. So you must make sure that you use the bathroom before lockup time." Beemer smiled at me apologetically. "I know that seems a bit harsh," he said, "but we can't have them roaming the streets at night getting into more trouble, can we?"

Marvel just looked at me.

I got to my office at about nine-fifteen. Jo was already there at her desk, typing up some invoices. She looked up. "Good morning," she said, and then, in a surprised tone, "Well, good morning, Marvel."

"Wha's up?" Marvel said.

"Jo, I'd like you to drive Marvel back to my place as soon as you finish your typing. He's going to be staying with me for a while." I took my May Company credit card from my wallet and tossed it on the desk. "Stop and get him a few shirts, a couple pairs of pants, including blue jeans, some shorts, and a couple pairs of sneakers—you know, Puma or Adidas or Reebok or whatever is in this year."

I riffled through my phone messages, aware that Jo was staring at me. Then I went back into my own little cubbyhole. She followed me, holding the credit card.

"Have you flipped out?"

"I don't want to discuss it."

"Well, I do. Did you take him to Saint Stephen's?"

"I did. And took him out of there just that fast. For God's

sake, he's just a little boy. I couldn't leave him in that—mausoleum."

"Are you going to keep him?"

"Jo, he's not a puppy that followed me home."

"Look, this is really noble and admirable of you, but you're taking on a lot of responsibility here."

"You think I don't know that? But I just couldn't leave him at Father Beemer's. You had to be there."

Her eyes twinkled. "Are we going to change the sign on the door to 'Saxon and Son'?"

"May you die the Death of a Thousand Cuts," I said.

She started out, then turned back to me. "I really think this is a terrific thing you're doing. Really. I just wonder if you've thought it all the way through."

"No," I said, "but I'm setting aside fifteen minutes next November to do that."

Jo smiled. "You're not so tough, you know."

"Tough enough to lick you and a couple of your friends," I said.

The fact is, I felt tough enough to do just about anything. I was still disoriented from my quick decision to keep Marvel with me for a while. I didn't know how it would turn out or even how I'd feel next week or next month about it, but if I thought everything out before acting I'd probably be a richer and happier man today. I was also stretched rather thin from the night before with Jennifer, and if anyone with my normally sunny disposition might be said to be feeling mean, this was the morn of my mornings. It was the ideal time for me to be doing what I was about to do as I found myself driving down Santa Monica Boulevard for the second time in an hour.

The address I'd gotten from Father Beemer the day before turned out to be a large white apartment complex that had been converted to condominiums several years earlier by a canny owner. It was between Santa Monica and Melrose Avenues, an off-white pseudocolonial of the type built in profusion in West Hollywood during the sixties. The sign on the front archway said FALCONWOOD, one of those non sequiturs used to name Los Angeles apartment buildings. There were a few For Sale signs stuck in the sloping lawn in front of the jacaranda trees and tropical bushes that hugged the stucco side of the building.

I parked my car across the street, hitched up the artillery in my armpit, and climbed the eight steps from the sidewalk to the double glass doors. There was a directory just outside the doors, and I found that the apartment I wanted was number 26. Inside the doors was an enclosed patio, complete with the usual scraggy palm trees, kidney-shaped swimming pool with detached spa, and sun-faded plastic deck chairs, the kind that left little striped welts all over your swimsuit-clad body when you sat in them for too long. From what I could see, all the apartments had doors that opened onto the patio, the second floor sporting a balcony that completely encircled the building. All the apartments on the first floor had numbers under twenty, so I reasoned that number 26 would be on the second floor. I climbed the metal staircase to the balcony and walked around it to the rear of the patio, where I found the door I wanted. I looked around. The whole place seemed deserted, which often happens on weekday mornings in apartment buildings. Places like this were a burglar's paradise, and though I didn't want to steal anything, I took advantage of the desertion of the moment and went to work on the lock with a set of picks I often use for that kind of operation. It took me about twenty seconds to get the door open; these places were long on phony atmosphere but fairly short on security.

I swung the door open quickly, the .38 in my hand, but the living room was empty, quiet. It was furnished sparsely with thrift shop and discount-house pieces, most of it more appropriate for the patio than the living room: a canvas butterfly chair stretched over a wrought-iron frame, a Formica table that had gone out of style in the fifties, a few rattan and wicker tables and some dinette chairs. There was an expensive stereo, though, and a small color TV with a VCR. I stood in the open doorway a second to get my bearings and then went in, closing the door quietly behind me. On one of the rattan tables there was a stack of handwritten papers held together with a staple, and a black leatherette notebook. With the end of the gun I flipped the book open and saw names, dates, places, money amounts. It was a trick book, as I had suspected.

Off to one side was a small dinette with no furniture in it, connected with a kitchen that looked as though no one had cooked a meal there for a long time. On the other side of the room was a hallway. I tiptoed past a small unclean bathroom in the hallway and into the bedroom. The door was open.

The bed was two twin box springs put together and topped with a king-size mattress; there was no bedstead or headboard, and the twin box springs rested on the floor, making ridges in the cheap apartment carpeting. Tony Haselhorst was asleep under a yellow sheet and a garish Mexican blanket, his acne looking more fiery in the daylight than it had under the fluorescent streetlights on the boulevard. He was apparently nude, on his back, one arm thrown up over his head. He was snoring softly. I went over to the bed, knelt down, and very gently touched his lips with the gun muzzle. He stirred fretfully, and I pressed a bit harder. He opened his eyes, blinked, then opened them again very wide, and when he started to say something I put the barrel of the .38 all the way into his mouth.

"Nn-gah nn-gah nnn-gah," he said. It was one of the better Bert Lahr impressions I'd heard in a long time.

"Sorry it's only two inches, Tony, but it's the best I can do."

He made about a quarter-inch effort to sit up and then thought better of it and lay back down on the pillow, the gun in his mouth, his eyes round, terrorized. His nose was swollen and purplish-red and there was a nasty scrape on the side of his face, and I knew I'd put those marks there on the street two nights before, and that made me feel good. In his fright his skin was even pastier than usual.

"Just give me the smallest reason to hurt you, Tony. Understand?"

He couldn't talk with the gun in his mouth so he blinked his eyes.

"Good boy," I said. "Now I'm going to ask you some questions, and you're going to answer them, and if I don't like your answers I'm going to take out some of your teeth with this thing, and when you have no teeth left I'm going to blow a big hole in the back of your head from the inside. Understand?"

Blink.

"All right now. I understand you knew Robbie Bingham."

He did Bert Lahr again.

"Is that a yes?"

He blinked.

"Was he one of your stable?"

The eyes opened wider and he made a similar noise, but it was different enough that I took it to be a no. I checked this out with him and he blinked again. He was having a little trouble breathing through his swollen nose. I didn't really care.

"Now I'm going to take this out of your mouth just far enough so you can talk to me, and if you don't talk nice I'm going to put it back and I'm going to be gentle about it. *Capeesh?*"

Blink. Blink.

I withdrew the muzzle enough so that the barrel was just touching his lips. He gasped for breath and I was kind enough to give him a few seconds.

"How did you know Robbie?"

"From the street," he croaked. "I know all the boys on the street."

"How many of them are yours now?" I said.

"I don't understand you."

I tapped his mouth lightly with the gun, and he whimpered.

"Six," he said. "I got six, without Marvel. Jesus, can I at least sit up?"

"I'm not Jesus, and no you can't," I said. "Why was Robbie afraid of you?"

"How the fuck should I know?"

I put the gun back in his mouth and waggled it around a little. I guess the metal must have hit a filling, because his whole body came up off the mattress convulsively, then sank back down, almost as if he were trying to disappear into it. I took the gun out. "Come again?"

He felt for the injured filling with his tongue and shuddered a bit. "I was trying to get him to come to work for me," he said.

"Why? Why Robbie?"

He shrugged. "He was pretty. He did well. I wanted a piece of the action. Look, I'm not the only—there were three or four guys who wanted Robbie."

"Names and addresses?"

He hesitated for a few seconds and I put the gun barrel back against his mouth. Not a love tap. I took it away. "Names and addresses?"

"Uh, Sonny G.—that's all I know him by. Jerry Grafton. A spade name of Whizzer something."

"Where do I find them?"

"Jesus, we weren't on come-to-dinner terms. They live around here someplace, I don't know."

"But what I hear is that you're the one Robbie was scared of. Why?"

Another pause, and then Haselhorst said, "I told him if he didn't start working for me it'd be his ass."

"So he refused you, and you snuffed him as a lesson to some of the other boys who wouldn't cooperate with you, make you the king pimp of Santa Monica Boulevard?"

"No, you got it wrong," he said. "He wasn't no use to me dead."

"If you didn't do him, who did?"

"How should I know? Look, everyone on the street is scared shitless as it is. Nobody knows who done it."

"Maybe the police will ask you nicer. The worst they'll get you for is pandering. You ought to be out in three or four years."

"You cocksucker," he said.

I pushed the gun in his mouth. "You'd know more about that than I would," I said. He gagged. "By the way, I understand you want to kill me. I think that'd be a real bad idea."

"Nn-gah nn-gah," he said. I took the gun out of his mouth.

"I was mad," he said, licking his lips. "That was just talk."

"It better be," I said. "I've made sure that if anything happens to me the police know who to talk to."

"I got no organization, man. I'm just one guy trying to make a buck."

"You are filth and scum," I said, "and if I ever see your face again on the street I'm going to come back and finish the job. Understand?"

He didn't have a gun in his mouth this time, but he just blinked anyway.

I straightened up and backed away from him, still pointing the .38 at him, trained on his middle. "You can consider yourself an official suspect in the Bingham killing," I said. "In my book, anyway."

"Your book may never get read," he said. I thought that was a pretty snappy comeback for a naked, terrified, pasty-faced pimp.

"Nevertheless," I said. I put my weapon back into my shoulder holster and turned my back on him. All right, sometimes I'm not as smart as other times.

I heard the covers rustle and turned back around to see he'd gotten out of bed and had his hand in the drawer of the nightstand. I covered the distance in three short strides and kicked the drawer shut on his fingers. He yelped in pain, and before he could remove his hand from the drawer I hit him on the side of the neck as hard as I could. Again, I was getting sloppy; I'd aimed for his jaw.

The effect was the same. He slammed back into the wall between the bed and the nightstand, and I fisted him hard in the stomach, my knuckles making a satisfying smack against his bare skin. He doubled up, gasping for air, and this time my blow landed where it was headed—and it hurt my hand like hell. I've been around long enough to know that when you punch a guy in the jaw, your fist is going to hurt almost as much as his jaw will. Mr. Haselhorst was beyond triumph, however. The punch snapped his head around sideways and I feared I had broken his neck. He slid down the wall into a sitting position, blood pouring out of his mouth, his rather inconsequential genitals exposed by his splayed knees. I hugged my fist under my other arm and hoped he wouldn't get up. He didn't.

I went to the splintered drawer and opened it to find a chromium-plated .32 pistol, not much more than a Saturday night special. He would have had to get awfully close with that to do any damage. I shook my head. Being a scumbag pimp is bad enough, but being an amateur scumbag pimp was almost unforgivable. I didn't touch the gun but left the drawer open wide. Then I went back into the living room.

I looked through his trick book and jotted down some names and dates, the most recent ones. I noted Marvel's name a couple of times, and for a moment I had the urge to go back inside and really do a job on Tony Haselhorst. I resisted the impulse. Every once in a while I play it smart. When I had gotten all the information I needed I took some toilet paper from the bathroom and lifted up the phone so as not to leave any prints. I called the police and told them there'd been an accident, gave them the address and a phony name, and suggested that when they come they bring someone from the vice squad with them. Then I left the trick book open on the Formica table, putting a can of beer on top of it to make sure the police noticed, and left as quietly as I'd come.

My hand was really hurting and starting to swell. I flexed my fingers and wrist enough to know it wasn't broken, but it was painful anyway, so I stopped at the nearest convenience store and bought an outrageously expensive bag of Party Ice and a newspaper. I put the newspaper on the passenger seat of my car, set the ice on top of it, and kept my right hand immersed in the ice whenever I didn't need it to shift. Just one of the prices one pays for driving a sports car.

I headed west on Santa Monica and when I got to the edge of Beverly Hills I cut over to Wilshire and parked in the Delacort's parking lot. It was a warm day and I didn't want to wreck my seat covers, so I dumped the ice on the ground and went into the store and asked for the art department.

Kevin Brody was hunched over a drafting table in a room that held eight of them, so concentrating on what he was doing that he didn't realize I was there until I peered over his shoulder at his drawing: an impossibly thin, imperious-looking woman wearing a stylish suit.

"Very nice," I said, and he jumped.

"Mr. Saxon. What are you doing here?"

"Take a break, Kevin, I have to talk to you."

He checked his watch. "I usually don't go to lunch until twelve-thirty."

"Well, today you're going to lunch now," I said. "On me."

We walked down Wilshire to Beverly Drive and then south to a little coffee shop. With his mincing gait and his makeup and earrings Kevin was making me acutely uncomfortable walking beside him. I hoped no one I knew from the movie business was going to walk into that coffee shop.

Kevin ordered a salad and a diet soda, and I asked for a roast beef sandwich and coffee, and when the bored waitress had gone away I said, "Why didn't you tell me about Tony Haselhorst?"

Under his pancake Kevin blanched. "Who?" he said carefully.

"Come on, Kevin, I'm in no mood. Tony Haselhorst is a pimp who'd been hassling Robbie to work for him and threatened him in the bargain. I can't believe Robbie didn't tell you."

Kevin didn't meet my gaze. "He may have said something, now that you mention it."

"Now that I mention it!" That was said so loudly several of the patrons looked over at us and smirked, obviously thinking they were watching a lover's spat. "Why didn't you tell me about this the first day in my office?"

"I didn't think it was important."

His body language gave him away. I said, "Kevin, you're lying to me."

He looked up at me, his eyes all squinched up from trying not to cry. I said, more quietly, "Why are you trying to protect Tony Haselhorst?"

"God damn it!" he whispered, emphasizing the *damn*.

"Kevin, there's been a murder committed. It's your duty to be completely open and aboveboard with me."

He took the kind of deep breath one takes before diving off the high board, before jumping off the ski jump, before hopping in to skip a rope being twirled by two other people. Then he said, "I told you Robbie and I loved each other."

I nodded.

"And that except for his tricks we were monogamous. Well . . . that wasn't exactly the truth."

He stopped as our lunches arrived, looking accusingly at the waitress, who was, after all, just doing her job. When she was gone he said, "I'm very sexy, Mr. Saxon. That is, I need a lot of sex. I would have preferred monogamy, with the one I loved. That would have been my first choice. But Robbie—he was out on the streets a lot, and sometimes when he came home there just wouldn't be anything left."

"So you had Haselhorst provide you with a boy whenever you felt the need?"

"I'm not proud of it."

"Couldn't you have found someone on your own?"

"I didn't want to get *involved,* I just wanted to party. You know, like you married straights do. You want to avoid emotional entanglements with another woman so you hire a hooker."

"But you were doing it with the money Robbie was selling himself to earn!" I said with disgust.

Kevin looked as sad as a person could look, because he was looking within and not enjoying the view. "That was the hell of it; like a vicious circle."

"So you were afraid if you blew the whistle on Haselhorst. . . ?"

Kevin nodded. "He wouldn't let me see Brian anymore."

I put my sandwich down without taking a bite. "Brian? Curly hair, works the same corner that Robbie did?"

He looked stunned. "You know Brian?"

"I know Brian," I said. I was tired. It had been a rough morning. "Good-looking guy."

Kevin nodded.

"Good-looking enough that you wanted Robbie out of the way so you and Brian could make it a little more permanent?"

He started to cry openly and shake his head. "I wouldn't do that," he said, "I couldn't do that."

I stood up and threw a ten-dollar bill on the table to cover the cost of lunch. "Probably not," I said, "but isn't it scary, Kevin, when you look in the mirror to do your makeup—and there isn't anybody there?"

Brian was right where I expected him to be, at the corner of Garden and Santa Monica. I pulled up alongside the curb and leaned over and opened the door for him. He got in.

"More talk?" he said.

I drove the car around the next corner and parked.

"Oh, this time you're looking for a little action?"

I reached out and grabbed his shirtfront and pulled him close. "You little bastard," I said, "why didn't you tell me you were tricking with Kevin Brody?"

"You didn't ask me. Besides, private eyes and whores have something in common: we never reveal the name of a client."

"I paid twenty-five dollars for information that I didn't get," I said.

"I'm a whore," Brian said. "You want information, go to the public library. And let go of my shirt—I told you, rough stuff costs more than twenty-five."

"You don't know what rough stuff is."

"I love it when you're butch," he said sardonically.

I let go of him and he leaned insolently back against the door. "Got a cigarette, Mr. Saxon? Oh, I forgot, you're trying to quit."

"You have a pretty good memory when you want to, don't you?"

"Look, I didn't mention Kevin because I didn't want to get involved, okay? I told you, minding my own business keeps me healthy."

"You mean you didn't tell me because maybe you wanted Robbie Bingham out of the picture so you and Kevin Brody could set up housekeeping."

"Don't make me ralph," he said. "Kevin is a nasty little queen, and I wouldn't have anything to do with him if he didn't pay me to. But if you want to try and make that stick, be my guest. I should warn you, though; I've got a friend on this street, and he'll take a pretty dim view of your hassling me like this."

"And I should warn you," I said with an amount of relish that, in hindsight, makes me ashamed of myself, "that even as we speak, your 'friend' is probably trying to explain to the cops why he has both a trick book and an unregistered firearm. And he's doing it through what I imagine is a broken jaw."

The insolent smile faded. "You are a mean son of a bitch, aren't you?" he said.

I leaned across him and opened the door he was leaning against so that he almost fell out onto the sidewalk. "And don't ever forget it," I said.

I pulled into the parking lot behind my office building and got out of the car. A youngish-looking man with thinning sandy hair and a Palm Springs tan got out of a dark blue Olds Cutlass and came wandering over to me. "Are you Mr. Saxon?" he said in a kind of tight-jawed way that made me think he'd just finished a set of tennis with Muffy and Binky and Skip. "My name is Ted Lawton, sergeant, Beverly Hills PD." He showed me his shield. "Can we talk in your office?"

130

"Sure, follow me."

As we were going up the stairs he said, "It was locked, so I decided to wait downstairs. It's such a nice day."

"Lovely," I said bitterly, unlocking my office door. I stood aside to let him enter, and together we went through the reception area to my back room.

"May I sit down?"

I laughed. "They grow them polite in Beverly Hills. We're not used to that here in Hollywood. Sure, make yourself comfortable."

He sat on the leather sofa and crossed his legs carefully so as not to disturb the crease in his gray slacks. He was wearing a blue blazer with gold buttons and a solid silver-blue tie against his pink button-down shirt.

"Speaking of that," I said, "aren't you a bit off base this far east?"

"Well, sometimes our work takes us far afield, just like yours. You get a little off base yourself at times, I'm told."

"Oh? By whom?"

"Lieutenant DiMattia, for one. Lieutenant Douglas of West Valley, for another."

"Two buddies," I said. "And now I have another one from Bev Hills, no less. It must be my charm."

"No, I think it's your nose. You seem to be sticking it into our case."

"Why, Sergeant Lawton, whatever could you mean?"

"Let's not be cute, Mr. Saxon. You're investigating the Robbie Bingham—Steven Brandon bombing. That's not nice. That's the kind of thing that loses licenses."

I didn't say anything for a minute. Then I offered to whip up a pot of coffee.

"No, thanks," he said. He was so damn affable it was making me nervous. "Maybe we could share information."

"Maybe," I said.

"What've you got?"

"You said share, Sergeant. What have *you* got."

"I asked you first. Besides, I have a badge, and that makes me decide who shares with whom."

I shrugged. "I'm sure you know as well as I do that there are about a million people who'd like to get Steven Brandon out of the way."

His blond brows knitted. "Steven Brandon? He was just an unlucky bystander."

"You think so?"

"I know so. He's a respected citizen."

"And respected citizens don't get murdered?"

"Not nearly so often as whores and faggots. We're playing the percentages here."

"You must have bet the Red Sox in the sixth game of the Series," I said.

"As a matter of fact, I did."

"Learn from your mistakes," I said.

"Mr. Saxon, you haven't told me anything."

"I don't have much to tell you," I said. "You might check out Bingham's roommate."

"We've already done that. We're not stupid."

"Oh," I said. I waited.

"You must not be worth a pitcher of warm piss as a detective if that's all you've got."

"No, that's not all, but anything else I might give you would just waste your time."

"Suppose," he said pleasantly, "you let me be the judge of that."

"Fine. There's a hustler name of Brian—no last name that I know of, works the southeast corner of Santa Monica and Garden—that you might like to chat with. And I believe that you'll find a pimp named Haselhorst currently in residence at the Hollywood station house taking his meals through a straw. If you're insisting that Steven Brandon had nothing to do with any of this, that's about all I can tell you."

"I'm not insisting," he said, "but it's my gut hunch and I'm going with it. I used to be on the San Francisco force. I know these fags. They're slime. Not one of them has the moral values of a sewer rat. They have sex indiscriminately, spread filth and disease, and to a man—and I use the word loosely—they're on drugs. They fight like bitches in heat, there's not a one of them I'd trust as far as I could throw him, and I can tell you they're all as vicious and spiteful as they come. And as far as I'm concerned they can all kill each other off with my blessing. But I've got a job to do and I'm doing it and trying not to let my own feelings get in the way."

"What a guy," I said.

"Who is your client, Mr. Saxon?"

"Now, you know I don't have to tell you that."

"I know. But it'd be nicer if you did."

"We can't have everything, Sergeant."

He stood up, adjusting his clothing. The jacket was tailored so snugly around his wiry frame that I was sure he wasn't carrying a weapon under it. My guess was that he was wearing an ankle gun. "Perhaps not," he said. "But if I find that you're withholding information from me, or if I find you in our way at any time, I'm going to have you. For brunch. You, your license, and your little pink ass. Something to think about, hmm?"

I rose with him and walked him to the outer door. "You know, Sergeant, I've been around quite a bit, both as a private investigator and as an actor. I'm sure you knew that." He nodded. "And the more I see of the world, the more I'm struck by how perfectly it's been organized: the balance of nature, the food chain, the ocean evaporating into the clouds and then the rain irrigating the fields. But one thing strikes me as a strange imbalance."

"Oh? And what might that be?"

"I can never understand why there are not enough horses to go with all the horses' asses in the world."

For just a second the icy cool of the man was penetrated and his blue eyes turned the color of granite. I understood why he'd made sergeant.

"We'll talk further," he said.

I was so glad. It gave me something to look forward to.

12

I turned on my answering machine and heard Steven Brandon's no-nonsense voice telling me that he'd checked out of the hospital and gone back home to Malibu and that I should call him there. I also had a message from Jennifer London.

I knew my priorities. I called Jennifer.

"You must think I'm terrible," she said.

"Not at all. It's happened to me on occasion. Don't take it so hard."

"I feel so rotten."

"Jennifer, we went through all this last night. There's nothing to feel rotten about."

She paused. "I'd like to make it up to you."

I laughed. "It doesn't work that way," I said. "You don't have to make it up to me. But I would like to see you again."

"Tonight?" she said.

"I don't know," I said. "I'm in the middle of this case now—"

"I don't blame you," she said. "I wouldn't want anything to do with me, either."

"I just said I wanted to see you again."

"You're just being nice. You're a very nice man."

"I'm not that nice. I want to be with you again, but things are kind of up in the air with this investigation."

"Maybe late. Come over late. Midnight. Whenever you finish."

There was real desperation in her voice that I was finding hard to understand. I didn't let it worry me—it had been a while since a woman as beautiful as Jennifer London was desperate for me. I said, "You're making me an offer I can't refuse, Jennifer. Look, why don't I call you tonight? See how my evening is going."

"I'll be here," she said, and she sounded very small and vulnerable on the other end of the phone, and that particular sound just pushes my buttons.

I took a few minutes to think about it after I hung up, and then I returned Steven Brandon's call.

"You got something to tell me?" he said.

"I haven't found the killer yet. I have a lot to tell you, though."

"Can you come out here now?" he said.

I looked at my watch. It was just past two.

"To Malibu?"

"I'm not exactly mobile these days. Sure, to Malibu."

I sighed. "Give me an hour."

I called Jay Dean at Triangle. "What are you doing for dinner?" I said.

"I've got a taping tonight but I could cut loose for an hour at about six. Why?"

"I need to pick your brain."

He hesitated, and I heard him puffing on his pipe. "It's a little late in the game for me to be putting my ass on the line," he finally said, "even for a friend."

"I won't attribute any quotes to you. But I just have to get a handle on this thing."

"All right," he said, "I'll meet you at the Mexican place across the street. But I don't guarantee I won't tell you to mind your business."

"This is my business, Jay," I reminded him, "but feel free not to answer any questions."

He sighed. "See you at six."

"Thanks, Jay."

Then I called my house and talked to Jo. The shopping expedition had gone well, and Marvel seemed more relaxed now that he'd been rescued from both Tony Haselhorst and Father Beemer's halfway house. I had interrupted a game of

Crazy Eights, apparently. "Jo, I have to go out to Malibu, and then tonight I've—got other things to do. But I'll stop by about four or so to change. Can you stay until then?"

"Pick up a pizza on the way," she told me. "Marvel has already eaten just about everything here that isn't still moving."

"You got it," I said. I hung up and made out a grocery list, full of unfamiliar things like peanut butter and milk and cookies and frozen burritos. I hadn't yet adjusted to being the father of a bouncing one-hundred-and-thirty-pound boy. I also made myself a big note on my calendar for the next day to start calling around for information on special schools. I shook my head in disbelief. Pretty soon I'd find myself spending Sunday at Disneyland.

I jumped onto the Hollywood Freeway, took it north to the San Fernando Valley, then took the Ventura Freeway westward to the Malibu Canyon exit and took the winding road through the hills to the Pacific Coast Highway. From there it wasn't too far to the Colony, an enclave of exclusive and horrendously expensive beachfront homes where many of the show business elite went to hide away and play. The questioning I got from the guard at the Colony entrance was only a bit more rigorous than the one I'd had to endure to get my private investigator's license.

When I finally reached Steven Brandon's home I was met at the door by a roly-poly little Swedish woman in a gray housekeeper's uniform. Her cheeks, bosom, arms, legs, and behind were all equally round, and she had merry twinkling blue eyes. She was what I wish my grandmother had looked like. I was expected, obviously, and she led me out onto the redwood sun deck where Steven Brandon was sprawled out on a poufy, comfortable-looking lounger. He wore white canvas duck pants and expensive leather thong sandals, and a terry-cloth beach jacket was draped over his shoulders. The bandages on his face and neck were smaller than they had been when I'd first seen him in the hospital, but the arm-and-shoulder cast was still in evidence. He waved me around to his right side and motioned to a chair. Next to him was a telephone on a long cord reaching from the living room with at least three different lines on it. Attempted murder victim or no, the telephone was an extension of the Hollywood big shot's anatomy, and he was loath to be more than two feet away from it at any time.

"You want something to drink?" he said loudly. "They told me no booze for a while because of the concussion, so I'm drinking orange juice. But there's no reason why you should suffer." Then, even louder, "Inger!"

Inger, the grandmotherly little housekeeper, came rolling out and I asked for a beer. She couldn't have possibly have been as delighted about it as she acted.

"So!" Brandon said. It was almost accusatory.

"I've been at it almost every minute, Mr. Brandon. I found several motives for someone to kill Robbie Bingham, although none of them seem terribly strong. I haven't found anyone who seems to want to kill you."

"What are you saying? That the cops are right, I was just in the wrong place at the wrong time?"

"Not necessarily."

"You think I'm wasting my money with you?"

"I'm not ready to say that just yet."

"Sure—you're making a good buck from me."

"Mr. Brandon, I managed to get along with my life quite nicely before I ever met you. I'm not going to blow smoke up your ass for a lousy three hundred a day."

"Spare the righteous indignation, will you? Am I murder bait or not?"

"Can I tell it my way?"

He took a slug of orange juice and made a baleful face.

Inger reappeared with my beer—Tecate, with an iced pilsner glass and a lime wedge beside it on the tray. I thanked her and poured while she bustled away. I waited for more arguments from Brandon, but when none came I started talking.

"Everyone I've spoken to seems to think that Triangle would fold up and sink like the *Andrea Doria* if anything were to happen to you."

"That's bullshit. There's plenty of capable people there that can do what I do."

"They all seem to think that you walk on water. Even though they're jealous of you, it appears their job security is more precious to them than their jealousies. Does that sound right?"

"I suppose."

"The word around town is that you're getting other offers. Are you considering them?"

"I'm always open, that's no secret. But I put too much into Triangle to leave them hanging. I'd make sure everything was going to run smoothly before I left."

"Does that mean you'd choose your own successor?"

He glanced off at the waves. "Let's say I would make strong suggestions."

"And who would you pick?"

He smiled. "Who would *you* pick?"

"If I were aiming for artistic integrity, Sanda Schuyler. If I wanted to make a lot of money, Irv Pritkin. And if I wanted a well-oiled, smooth-running organization, I suppose Stu Wilson."

"Not bad," he said. "That's pretty much the way I look at it."

"So all three of them figure they'd have a shot at the top job if you were out of the way?"

"I haven't made any recommendations yet. And if I'd been blown to hell by that bomb I wouldn't have had the chance."

"So you're saying none of the three had a motive to kill you?"

"No, they all do—and they don't. Jesus Christ, how do I know? Maybe it's somebody who's not with the network."

"Like who?"

"I don't know that, either."

"It seems to me we ought to be paying a little more attention to your personal relationships."

"I don't have any," he said, "besides Raina."

"You don't go out with other women?"

"Sure I do. Once, twice at the most. Half the time I don't even screw them. They're doing a show or a film for the network and need the kind of publicity they get when they go places with me, and I need a date for all those boring damn parties. I'd have to look at my appointment calendar even to tell you what their names are."

"I'm going to ask you a question you're not going to like."

"I haven't liked any of them so far. Why should this one be different?"

"Have you ever had a homosexual relationship?"

He looked at me, his blue eyes squinted against the sun coming off the water. "There's about a thousand women in this town'll tell you I'm straight."

"References aren't very helpful here," I said. "Lots of people go both ways."

"Do you?" he said.

"Whether I do or not isn't germane to the problem, Mr. Brandon. However, to satisfy your curiosity, no, I don't."

"Well, I don't either," he said. Then he sighed. "I was with another man *once*. Several years ago. When I was still at Paramount. I was a production executive and he was a young actor on some picture or other. We were at a party one night; I'd been drinking. He came on to me. I thought, what the hell. I'm told that everyone, even the straightest of people, have a certain curiosity about getting it on with someone of their own sex, and I've always advocated having as many experiences as I can in different fields. I've jumped out of an airplane, I've scuba dived in shark-infested waters, I've climbed mountains—just to have the experience. Everyone should try everything at least once. It was intellectual curiosity, that's all."

"And was your curiosity satisfied?"

"That's why I only did it once. I decided it was okay but I liked women a lot better. Now is *your* curiosity satisfied?"

"Not quite," I said. "Could you give me the actor's name?"

"No, I could not," he said emphatically.

"Why not?"

"It's a waste of time. He got out of the business. He's living back east. New Orleans, I think."

"You keep in touch?"

"Christ, no. When I took the job at Triangle he wrote me a letter. Congratulations, the best rise to the top, all that. He's working in some boutique or other—or he was then. It was a long time ago and I never answered the letter and I never heard from him again."

"Did you keep the letter?"

He laughed at the absurdity. "I don't even keep love letters from women."

"Do you remember the boy's name, Mr. Brandon, or are you just not going to tell me?"

He ran his good hand over his face. He needed a shave. "It's a waste of time."

"It might be at that. Why not let me decide? That's what you're paying me for."

"It's a can of worms I'd just as soon not have opened again. Look, Saxon, this is a funny town, a funny business—you know that; you're in it. Everything is typecasting, everyone has a label. Bogart slugged a guy in a nightclub fighting over a panda and was branded a hardass and a hothead the rest of his life. It took Bob Mitchum twenty years to live down that pot-smoking business, and by the time he did everyone else was smoking it. Homosexuality is a strange thing here, even though half the actors I know walk a little lightly in their loafers. You try it once, you're a philosopher. Try it twice, you're a fag. Now, everyone knows this bomb thing was connected with a gay hustler from Santa Monica Boulevard in the other car. If it comes out that five or six years ago I had a one-nighter with another man, all of a sudden people start calling me the Fairy Prince. I've got enough trouble with guys taking swipes at me for being greedy or ambitious or unethical or ruthless without having rumors circulating about my masculinity."

"Would you rather be dead?"

His mouth tightened. "What do you mean?"

"You're paying me a lot of money to find out if someone tried to kill you, and if so, who. You don't have any friends, your co-workers think you're Jesus of Nazareth, and you've got so many women it would take me until we're both old men to check all of them out. This is an area I'd like to explore just slightly. You tell me the guy's name and where I can find him, and I'll check it out discreetly and quietly without bringing your name into it. It's probably nothing, but are you willing to gamble your life on it?"

He stared out at the waves crashing some hundred yards away on the beach. He looked very sad and very young and not at all like the most famous Hollywood wunderkind since James Aubrey. He said, "This is damn embarrassing."

"I'm sorry. I don't want to make you uncomfortable. But I don't want to make you dead, either."

We both stared out at the waves. Loving the ocean as I do I couldn't help envy him, sitting here looking out at the water, watching the porpoises jump and play—and watching the nubile California beach bunnies jump and play as well—drinking in the smell of sea air and watching the sunset every evening. He had earned this house and this life-style by hard work and rugged tenacity and by using his wits and his intuition, and he didn't want a youthful indiscretion to bring it all down around his ears. I finished the Tecate.

"Another one?" Brandon said. "Come on, you might as well, it's a warm day."

"I don't want to trouble Inger," I said. "I don't want to trouble you, either, Mr. Brandon, and if you won't tell me, I'll understand. I just think it's worth a few phone calls, that's all."

The telephone rang and one of the buttons started flashing. He called out, "Hold all my calls, Inger," and then when the ringing stopped and the pulsating light changed to a solid glow, he turned and looked at me. "The boy's name was Dennis Pine," he said. "He just had a small part in some film at Paramount. It was at the wrap party on the set. I don't even remember what the picture was. Like I said, I'd had a lot to drink. He was flirting with me—Jesus, this sounds bizarre!—and he was very slim and blond and pretty like a girl—and I went home with him."

"And?"

"What do you mean, 'and'?" he said angrily. "You want to know who did what to whom?"

"No," I said gently. "You spent the night?"

"Hell, no. We did what we did and then I got out of there. I told him I was straight and that we wouldn't be seeing each other again and asked him please not to call me or anything, and he said it was all right, that he understood, and I went home and took a very hot shower and pretty much forgot about it."

"You never saw him again?"

"A few months later he was doing another picture. I saw

143

him on the lot. We waved at each other and that was it. The next I heard from him was the letter when I moved over to Triangle. He said he'd quit the business because he couldn't make enough money and was into designing clothes for this shop in New Orleans. I threw the letter away and didn't answer it. That's it."

"You remember the name of the shop?"

"How am I supposed to remember that? It was five years ago." He knitted his brow. "Wait. It was some sort of gay name. Us, or something."

"Us?"

He looked up at me. "Ours. That was the name of the shop: Ours."

"In New Orleans?"

"Look, I don't want this stirred up again, Saxon, you understand me?"

"If I can't get what I need without stirring things up, I won't get it. All right?"

He shook his head wearily. "I did some checking up on you after I hired you," he said. "Word is that you're as honest as Abe Lincoln. It's a damn good thing."

"Why?"

"Because if you wanted to you could blackmail me for the whole enchilada with this. You could make me make you a star, if you wanted."

"I'd love to be a star, Mr. Brandon," I said. "Then I could quit being a private investigator and move next door to you here. But I'll do it on my own hook or not at all. I told you that once before."

"Yeah, I know," he said tightly.

"But you're lucky I am honest. And you're lucky Dennis Pine is honest, too, because it occurs to me that he could have done the same thing."

"It occurred to me, too."

"But he never attempted anything like that?"

"No," he said. "He never did. He was a sweet kid." He went within for a moment, in some far-off reverie. I didn't want to disturb him, so I left quietly. In the living room Inger intercepted me like a round little sheepdog and led me to the front door. As I turned to thank her I could see Brandon framed in the enormous glass door that led to the beachside deck. He had his good hand over his eyes, and though it was hard to tell from that distance, it looked as if he was crying.

○ 13 ○

I walked in laden with grocery bags from the market. I always hate it when the bag boy asks if I want paper or plastic. Life is too full of decisions as it is. On this particular day I had told him to surprise me, and apparently they had more plastic bags to get rid of than the old-fashioned paper kind, so here I was.

Marvel was watching his cartoons on the sofa and Jo was sitting in my favorite chair reading Raymond Chandler's *Lady in the Lake.*

"Isn't this the one they made into a movie where you never saw Philip Marlowe's face except in a mirror?" she said.

"That's right. Robert Montgomery and Audrey Totter."

"I haven't any idea who they are," she said.

"I find that to be a sad and tawdry admission." I looked at Marvel, who had barely glanced up at my entrance. "How you doin' there, slugger?"

"Awri'," he said. "You bring a pizza?"

"No. I got burritos instead. You like burritos?"

"They awri'," he said, and went back to cartoons.

"You're going to eat a frozen burrito?" Jo said, coming into the kitchen where I was putting away the food.

"Not while I live. I'm going out to dinner."

There was silence except for the rustling of plastic and the noise of the refrigerator door opening and closing as I finished putting away the comestibles. When I looked over at me she was looking very prim and tight-lipped. "What's your trouble, little bubble?"

"I think that stinks," she said.

"Frozen burritos? I agree. That's why I'm eating out."

"You know very well what I mean." She lowered her voice,

although the cartoons were so loud it's doubtful Marvel would have heard her if she'd screamed. "You got all noble this morning about keeping that child with you, and now you don't even have the decency to stay here with him."

I sighed, leaning against the refrigerator. It felt cool through my shirt. "I have a living to make, Jo," I said, "which, by the way, pays your salary. I don't punch a time clock; that's not how I work. I'm having dinner with Jay Dean at Triangle to get some more information on Steven Brandon."

"Good," she said. "And then you're coming back to spend the evening with Marvel?"

I bit my lip. It was what Jo often refers to as my caught-in-the-cookie-jar look, so she recognized it right away.

"You're going to let that kid sit here and OD on television while you're out with some bimbo?"

"Jo," I said in what I thought was my most reasonable tone, "she's someone connected with the case, too."

"That Jennifer?"

"Yes, that Jennifer."

She looked at me coldly. It was what I called her Death Ray look, and I was just as adept at recognizing her looks as she was mine.

"Jo, I'm only human."

"So is Marvel," she said. "He's a human being, and you're treating him like some new piece of furniture or a hunk of sculpture you've just acquired."

"That's not fair."

"Damn right it isn't. He's a scared, lonely, confused kid and he needs a little TLC. Some kind attention. Oh, you should've heard him this morning on the way home. Talking about how 'cool' you are for not leaving him at Father Beemer's. At least there he would have someone to talk to."

"Yeah," I said, "a sanctimonious priest and a kid with spiked hair who calls him a boogie."

"At least he calls him *something*," Jo said.

I didn't say anything. The Death Ray was robbing me of my powers of speech.

She said, "Well, you do what you've got to do." She tossed poor Raymond Chandler unceremoniously on the kitchen counter and he slid over the tile and into the sink, which fortunately was dry and empty.

"Easy," I said. "Books are your friends."

"I'm not sure you know the meaning of the word," she said. "I'll see you in the office in the morning. Try to wipe the lipstick off before you come in, okay?"

She went back into the living room and I heard her saying good-bye to Marvel, and she gave him her home phone number in case he got lonely and wanted to talk during the evening. I got a bottle of John Courage out of the refrigerator and had a sudden yen to bite off the cap, but I kept it under control and used the magenta bottle opener I had stolen years before from the Madonna Inn in San Luis Obispo. I felt like David Copperfield's stepfather.

Jo's door-slam put an abrupt period on my musings. I took a long pull on the beer, one of my favorites, and walked out into the living room and sat down next to Marvel on the sofa. He was watching something called "He-Man."

"I'll put your dinner on in a second," I said.

"Tha' be cool."

"Marvel, could we turn down the TV a little?"

He pointed the remote control at the set and sounds of carnage and the *bum-ba-pa-BUM!* music were muted. He looked at me expectantly.

"Well," I said.

What the hell, it was a beginning.

"Tomorrow I'm going to find out about getting you into a school. You think you'll like that?"

He shrugged. "I learn readin'?"

"First thing."

"Tha's good."

"Uh, I'm sorry I can't have dinner here with you," I said. He looked at me without blinking. "I have to work."

"Uh-huh. 'M I gonna stay here from now on?"

"We'll see," I said.

"Yeah," he drawled. "I know 'bout 'see.'"

"Would you like to?"

"I don' know." He glanced over at the TV and then back at me. "You wan' me to?"

"Uh, I guess—sure. If it works out."

"Uh-huh."

I looked at my watch. "Well, I've got to change," I said. "I'll put your burrito in the oven. There's milk and juice in the fridge."

"Uh-huh."

I stood up, taking another gulp of John Courage.

"You not be home too much."

"Well, I am sometimes," I said defensively. Then, "Look, Marvel, I should be home tonight about eight-thirty or nine," I said. "We can spend some time together then, okay? We'll talk—and I'll whip your butt at Crazy Eights. Is that a deal?"

"Tha's cool," Marvel said.

I went back into my bedroom, turned on the shower, and stripped out of my clothes. If I were going to spend much time talking with Marvel I'd have to write myself a monologue. He didn't give much back.

After my shower I bit the bullet and called Jennifer to tell her I wouldn't be able to see her tonight after all.

"I knew it," she said sadly. "You don't want to see me."

"Let's not replay that one, Jennifer. I'm in the middle of a case and until it gets straightened out, I won't have much free time."

"Oh, your case," she said. "How's it coming?"

"Slowly but surely."

"You know who did it yet?"

"No. If I knew, the case would be wrapped up."

"It was somebody tried to kill that poor kid, wasn't it?"

"That's what I'm going to try and find out tonight," I said.

"And that's going to take you until after midnight?"

"There are other considerations. I just can't make it tonight, that's all."

Her voice grew sharp. "It's another woman, isn't it?"

"No—"

"God damn men!" she said. "You're all alike. You've been with me, now you're bored and looking for new worlds to conquer."

"I *haven't* been with you, may I remind you. And I'm not seeing another woman. As a matter of fact I'm having dinner with someone from Triangle and then spending the rest of the evening with a fourteen-year-old boy."

"You didn't strike me as a switch-hitter," she said nastily, "but you can't ever tell these days. So who's this person you're having dinner with?"

I didn't think our relationship was quite at the stage that would require me to tell her with whom I was spending my time. I told her so.

Her tone softened. "I'm sorry. I'm just so terrified that the killer's going to be coming for me. That's why I'm so anxious for you to catch him." And then, kittenishly, "Forgive me?"

Being kittenish is cute when the practitioner is a kitten. When she's human and over the age of four it's a bit cloying. I was beginning to look forward to the prospects of an evening of Crazy Eights. Beautiful as Jennifer London was, I was starting to get a strange feeling about her.

"Sure," I said.

I finished dressing and went back out into the living room. The TV was still on, but Marvel was over by the wall looking at my record collection.

"You like jazz?" I said.

He shrugged. "Don' know what it is."

"It's great," I said. "A lot of jazz musicians are black." I could have bitten off the end of my tongue. The next thing you know, I was going to be telling him what a great ballplayer Jackie Robinson was and how Sidney Poitier was my favorite actor.

"In case you get bored with TV," I went on, "you might try listening to some of these."

"Which?"

"Well, let's see." I started looking through the LPs. Do you start a novice out on Miles Davis? I didn't think so. I took out a Louis Armstrong album and one by the Oscar Peterson trio, and after hesitating a moment I also selected an old Columbia Masterworks classic called *Ellington Uptown*. If anyone could listen to that and not get into it, his ear was irredeemably tin and there was not much more that could be done for him. I went to the record changer and stacked the records on the spindle, the Ellington first. "Just push this button, Marvel," I said. "In case you get bored with TV."

"Awri'," he said. "Could you bring back some choc'lit ice cream?"

I tried to remember the last time I'd had chocolate ice cream in my freezer. It eluded me. There was a subtle upheaval taking place in my well-ordered world, and Häagen-Dazs was spearheading the revolution. It was unsettling, to say the least.

I rode the halting elevator down to the garage beneath my apartment building, got into my car, and pointed the remote-control device at the security gate that kept unauthorized cars and pedestrians from roaming the garage at will. Nothing happened. I wasn't surprised. It was the third time in the last two months that the remote control had failed to open the gate. I had called the building's absentee manager along with most of the other tenants, and some mysterious gremlin with a screwdriver and a voltage regulator had come down and performed strange rites and the gate had worked for a week and then broken down again. There was nothing for it but that I get out of my car, walk over to the wall next to the gate and depress the emergency button in the control box on the wall, and then watch while the sliding metal gate rumbled open like the entrance to an enchanted castle in a fairy tale. I went back to my car, hurrying to put it in reverse and then in first gear so I could scurry out the up-sloping driveway before the gate closed on me. It was one more instance of the electronic age failing to live up to its glowing public relations.

Driving toward Burbank and my dinner with Jay Dean I realized how far out of my depth I was with my new responsibilities. I had no idea whether Marvel was really retarded or simply unlettered, but I knew I was going to have to stop treating him like a three-eyed, six-toed visitor from Saturn. He obviously knew what a stereo was and how to turn the oven on and off and how to go to the store, but so deep was his light buried that I was unsure how much more he really knew or was capable of learning. Case or no case, I was obligated to spend some time finding a school where he could fit in and where his potential could be explored and expanded, and I hadn't the foggiest notion of where to start. All right, Saxon, you're a private detective. If you wanted to find a certain kind of school, where would you look? Not the yellow pages. You'd call someone, right? How about your buddy, Bill Laven? When he wasn't suffering over the reports of the dismal doings of the Chicago Cubs he was on the board of several foundations that worked with the physically disabled. Not the same thing, but perhaps someone he knew would know someone else and . . . I'd call Bill in the morning.

The Valley-bound homeward rush on the San Diego Freeway was nothing short of horrendous, but there wasn't much I could do about it, so I joined the army of cars inching northward at Sunset Boulevard and occupied my mind with games, such as establishing the fact that seven of every ten cars on the freeway were driven by men, which then made me wonder about those reports that more than half the work force was female. And of those on their way home, only one woman out of fifteen was even worth flirting with. A man in an open convertible with no one to smile at was simply a guy with his hair mussed up. At the top of the Sepulveda Pass I could look down on the brown blanket of smog that lay across the entire San Fernando Valley, and my eyes began smarting in anticipation.

Being wise in the ways of Los Angeles freeways, I had allowed enough time to compensate for the traffic and arrived at the Mexican restaurant ten minutes early. The hostess, an Anglo teenager wearing a Mexican fiesta dress, insisted I wait until my entire party had shown up before taking a table, so I went into the bar and ordered a double margarita. When I am having dinner at a Mexican restaurant I always drink margaritas. I don't know why; I suppose it's a reflex action, the same way I always have a hot dog at Dodger Stadium and never *ever* anyplace else.

I had about half the salt licked off the rim of my glass when I heard a very familiar voice close to my ear saying, "Well, if it isn't Mr. Smartass!"

Scott Raney looked very angry when I turned on the stool, but his was still that we-have-nice-parting-gifts-for-you-anyway tone of the professional emcee, jovial and relentlessly cheerful.

"Hello, Scott," I said.

"Well, you certainly made me look like a horse's patoot!" he went on.

That wasn't exactly alchemist's magic, but I did feel I should say something nice. "I'm sorry. Sometimes my sense of humor is a little off the wall."

"Can you imagine my embarrassment when I told my producer I'd run into Hoot Gibson and he told me Hoot Gibson had been dead for years?"

I could imagine. He probably hadn't said he'd "run into" Hoot Gibson, but instead that Hoot Gibson was his very very very dear friend and that he'd had a cup of coffee with him just the other morning, which would have taken the embarrassment quotient to the tenth power.

"It was a bad joke," I said. "Will buying you a drink make up for it?"

"No, but it's a start." He climbed up onto the stool beside mine. "Who the hell *are* you, anyway?"

I told him. "And since I don't have a regular gig on a show that takes its time slot sixteen weeks in a row—"

"Seventeen," he corrected me. "Probably be eighteen when the next ratings book comes out."

"—I sometimes supplement my income by working as a private investigator." I gave him my card. He looked at it with little interest and stuck it in the pocket of his jacket. Either he was between tapings or he always wore pancake makeup to dinner.

"So that must mean you're working on something at Triangle. Let me guess: a little industrial espionage? No, I know—it's the Brandon bombing."

"That's pretty good," I said.

"You were asking me questions about Steven in the cafeteria. I just put two and two together. Well, how can I be of help to you?"

"I don't know," I said.

"Am I a suspect?"

"Would you like to be?"

He waved his hand breezily and consumed more than half of the vodka and tonic he'd ordered. "Hell, why not? I didn't do it, so it might be fun being a suspect."

"Okay," I said, "you're a suspect. Happy?"

"Damn right I'm happy," he said. "I make half a million dollars a year on 'Deal' for showing up twice a week, and that lets me make another two hundred or so big ones doing commercials and public appearances. They treat me like I'm Charlton Heston when it comes to getting good tables and not waiting in airport lines, and I get more ass than I know what to do with. What's not to be happy?"

"You're right," I said. "Then you'd have no reason to want Brandon dead."

"Other than the fact I'd probably get a better shake from someone else in his chair, no."

"Why do you think that?"

"Steven doesn't like me very much. He thinks I'm a lightweight. Well, maybe I am, but I'm smart enough to have parlayed no talent, a pleasant speaking voice, and a nice smile— courtesy of Murray Cooperstein, D.D.S.—into a pretty good living. So piss on Steven Brandon."

I raised my glass. "Piss on Steven Brandon."

He turned serious. "That doesn't mean I tried to kill him. If I were going to waste everyone who thinks I have no talent, this would be a ghost town."

"People have killed for less. You don't happen to own a BMW, do you?"

"As a matter of fact, yes. And a little three-fifty SL and a Toyota van for when I see my kids on weekends. I've got four kids, you know."

He pulled out his wallet and showed me his two girls and two boys. The boys looked like their father and the girls looked like Vanna White. Gene pools are strange and mysterious things.

"You have kids?"

I licked off the last of the bar salt from the rim of my glass.

"I'm not sure," I said. He whooped, taking it the wrong way, and I didn't feel like explaining about Marvel, so I let it go.

"Who else is a suspect?"

"Everyone who knows Brandon. Everyone who knows the boy who was killed. Everyone who might have seen a show on Triangle that offended them or hit too close to home or rubbed them the wrong way."

"That narrows it down to about two hundred million people," he said.

"And how many of them drive BMWs?"

"Son of a bitch, you *are* serious," he said.

"Sometimes my sense of humor deserts me."

He waved at the bartender for another drink. I put my hand over the top of my glass to indicate I wasn't ready. He said, "Did the killer drive a BMW?"

"Something like that."

"Well, half of executive row at Triangle does. It's what Mercedes used to be—a Yuppie status symbol."

"I think I read that somewhere," I said.

"But I'll tell you this much: Steven Brandon is one hard son of a bitch when it comes to contracts. I think I told you he's giving me a bad time. And he's just as hard on the people at the network as he is on talent and suppliers. I never much thought about murder, but I'm here to tell you Steven's a prime candidate. When you've got so much power that everyone's afraid of you, then a lot of people are going to want to see you dead."

"Are you afraid of him, Scott?"

"Damn straight I am! Look, I'm like anyone else: I want to get the best deal for myself. But I know if I push too hard, take one step too many, the son of a bitch will dump me faster than yesterday's halibut and hire someone younger, prettier, and even more vapid than I am for 'Deal of a Lifetime,' and I'll spend the rest of my life doing walk-ons on

'Hotel' and summer stock and in road companies of *The Odd Couple*. You bet your booties I'm afraid of him."

"My booties?" I said.

He looked grim. "Why are you always putting me down?"

"I'm sorry. I guess I'm jealous." Over his shoulder I saw that Jay had just come in and was standing at the entrance to the bar trying to adjust his eyes to the gloomy lighting. "A guy who makes almost a million a year and gets more ass than he can handle, who wouldn't want to be in your shoes? Or booties?"

He nodded. "I see what you mean," he said. Yes, he really did, he said that.

"So jealous, in fact, that I'm going to let you pay for the drinks." I pushed my bar tab toward him and said to the bartender in a loud, cheery voice, "Tell him about it, Juanito!"

I stood up and walked to where Jay Dean was waiting for me near the hostess station. "Does Scott Raney always talk like one more right answer and you get to play the bonus round?"

"Yes," Jay said. "If he ever stops, the caps fall off his teeth, the padding comes out of his jacket, and he has to go out and get a real job."

We were led to a booth near the back of the restaurant, and we both ordered margaritas before looking at the menu. When we had our drinks in front of us, Jay said, "What's up, Doc?"

"Jay, I'm sure you've figured out by now that I'm on Steven Brandon's case."

"Trying to find out if he was the intended victim?"

I nodded. "You've been at this network a hundred years. Give me a rundown."

"On Brandon?"

"No, I know all about him, and what else I need I can get

from the papers. I need some information on your executive row."

Jay lit his pipe. It was beginning to annoy me, especially since the smell of the sweet tobacco he smoked made me acutely aware of how much I wanted a cigarette. He said, "You know the definition of a network executive who talks about his bosses behind their backs? A real estate salesman in Van Nuys."

"I told you, this is all off the record. Also, I might remind you of that memo from the boss of bosses, Mr. Brandon himself, about cooperating with me."

"Name-dropper," he said. "All right, go ahead."

"Stuart Wilson."

"Stu and I are of an age and of an era. The reason he's bopped around to every studio and network in town while I stayed at Triangle is that Stuart says what he thinks and I say what's nice and safe. He's very defensive about his age, he knows his business better than anyone else at Triangle, but in his heart of hearts he'd like to bring back 'Mister Ed' and the Beaver."

"How does he get along with Brandon?"

Jay puffed. "Steven respects him because he's not afraid to call it like he sees it. So many people kiss Steven's ass I think it's refreshing for him to find someone who won't. However—and this is a big however—Stu is a pretty spiky guy sometimes."

"I've noticed."

"And sometimes it gets on Steven's nerves. As much as he hates yes-men, I think he'd like it more if Stu agreed with him at least once in a while."

"You feel Stu's job at Triangle is in jeopardy?"

"Everyone with VP after his name walks a tightrope every day."

"Wilson drive a BMW?"

"Yes," he said, "all the brass do. It's this year's car."

"Schuyler and Pritkin, too?"

"Yeah, I think so."

"Tell me about Irv Pritkin."

"You met him, you've seen it all. He lives in Encino, goes to temple, his kids play Little League and AYSO soccer. He's trying hard, but he's just not show business. He's an accountant, he thinks like an accountant, and in today's movie and TV business that means he'll be around a while."

"Isn't he Brandon's fair-haired boy?"

"Sure. Steven handpicked him for the network, and was only too happy to put him into a VP slot in programming. But Steven is a bottom-liner himself, and I think he'd be more comfortable with someone with a little more imagination in a creative programming post."

"You'd say then that Pritkin is shaky where he is?"

"I wouldn't call it shaky. But I wouldn't be surprised to find Irv Pritkin in business affairs rather than programming."

"You think that would bother him?"

"It'd bother me," Jay said, "but I'm not Irv. Look, when you're a programming VP there are perks that don't come with a calculator and slide rule."

"Such as?"

"Come on, Saxon, you know it as well as I do. What do you want, to hear me say it? Programming is glamour. It's power. People take you to lunch, to dinner, they give you Piaget watches for Christmas, they give you great tickets to Dodger games, once in a while they supply a willing and nubile maiden—"

"Does Irv Pritkin take time out from coaching Little League for hookers?"

"I don't know, never heard that about him. It's the principle of the thing. Business affairs hold the purse strings, but you don't even get a peek into that purse unless someone in programming orders a pilot or a series or a movie of the week. If I were a skinny, funny-looking guy who carries a calculator in his pocket and I found myself having lunch with Carol Burnett or Norman Lear or Burt Reynolds all of a sudden, I sure wouldn't want to go back into the stacks and figure out prize budgets for game shows."

"Does Pritkin know where he stands?"

He shrugged. "There was a staff meeting about a month ago—nobody under the rank of vice president—and Steven told Irv to use his imagination once in a while instead of his slide rule."

"In front of God and everybody?"

Jay Dean smiled. "God wasn't there—I told you, no one under the rank of network vice president. No deities were invited."

The waiter came to take our dinner orders. I chose the *camarones* in green sauce, which the menu assured me was the chef's own prize-winning recipe. Jay ordered a taco and enchilada combination. That's why he'd stayed at the network for so long—he avoided anything that might be controversial. We also ordered two more margaritas, and I thought, Jay being Jay, that was pretty racy when he had to go back to work that evening.

"Sanda Schuyler," I said.

"One of the brightest women I've ever met. She worked for me when she first came to Triangle, twelve or thirteen years ago. Wherever they put her, she shone like a new copper penny. Learned every facet—programming, sales, business affairs, even electronics and engineering. When we had a NABET strike a few years back Sanda functioned as our chief engineer while the rest of us execs pointed cameras and held cue cards. She made it to executive row about four years ago. Most of our hit shows came out of Sanda's brain, or at the very least from across her desk."

"I thought all the programming decisions were Brandon's."

"He can't make decisions on projects he doesn't see, and he turns down three-quarters of what he's pitched. So Sanda's batting average is really impressive."

Our food arrived. I don't know where the *camarones* had won a prize, but it must have been in a contest I wouldn't want to judge. Jay ate his combination plate with gusto. There's something to be said for circumspection, I suppose.

"How does it work?"

"You're a supplier," he said between forkfuls. "Universal, Lorimar, whoever. You have an idea, something you've come up with or that was submitted to you from outside. You'd like to do a network pilot on it, so you bring it to Sanda Schuyler. She works with you, develops it, hones it, makes it as slick and commercial and as saleable as she can, and most of the time you listen to her suggestions because she's got the best story mind in Hollywood since Irving Thalberg died. Then, when she thinks it's right, when she thinks it's ready, she takes it to Steven. And we're not talking running it up the flagpole, here, we're talking advocacy. It's her baby and she works for it, protects it, pitches and sells and bullies and cajoles and pleads. And Steven listens to her nine out of ten times because he knows how good she is. *All* the Triangle hits of the past four years came from Sanda Schuyler. A few flops, but even Keith Hernandez strikes out occasionally. The woman is uncanny, and Steven and everyone else in town knows it."

"If she's so good, why doesn't she go independent? Start her own production company? I'm sure she could sell to Triangle, or any of the other networks, if she's as good as you say."

"A couple of reasons. She likes the security of the network, for one thing. For another, she likes the power. Sanda's a lesbian, as I'm sure you know, and I think she gets off on having these rich, powerful men dancing to her tune. Also, I'm not sure she'd be that successful."

"Why in hell not?"

"Everyone's kinky in the business, Saxon, you know that—little boys, little girls, orgies, water sports, B and D—but they're fairly discreet about it. Sanda flaunts her sexual preference like a flag, and I think it makes a lot of people uncomfortable. In this industry women are for bedding, in thought if not in deed. When one comes along that you can't even have the fun of fantasizing about, it makes you nervous."

"It doesn't make *me* nervous."

"You're not a power broker, my friend. You and I, we take our fun where we find it. I've been married for twenty-eight years and my wife still turns me on, so I imagine you find it in more places than I do. But you understand me: a yes or a no, it's all the same to you. You're used to it. Hollywood big shots aren't. They don't know what to do with it."

"So you're saying Sanda Schuyler has reached as far as she's going to?"

"Not necessarily. People like that are valuable to a big shop like Triangle. I'd say that if Steven Brandon were to step down, there's a very good chance Ms. Schuyler would be running this network."

"So all three of them might have good reason to try to snuff Brandon?"

"Them and a hundred others. But yes, I'd say that was accurate."

I pushed my *camarones* around the plate until someone came to take them away and throw them in the garbage where they belonged. "Coffee?" I said. "Or how about a flan for dessert?"

He patted his stomach. "I'm watching it these days. You noticed I didn't have any chips and salsa."

"I wasn't watching what you were eating, but I understand," I said.

"Understand too about the confidentiality," he said without smiling. "You never talked to me, and if you say you did I'll deny it heatedly and it might get very unpleasant vis-à-vis your acting career."

I said quietly, "Are you threatening me, Jay?"

He smiled suddenly around the stem of his pipe. "We've been friends too long for that," he said. "I think . . . I'm begging you."

There was no traffic to speak of going home, especially on the long haul out Sunset Boulevard. Once again, as I did so often, I thought about getting an apartment closer to town and saving myself the hassle of an hour's drive to work each way, but I liked the remoteness of the Palisades, I liked the proximity to the beach, I liked the fact that not too many industry people lived out there compared to Beverly Hills or Malibu or the more expensive sections of the San Fernando Valley. It also gave me time to unwind after a hard day playing detective. And to think.

I had a lot to think about on this particular evening. If I turned up any more suspects in this case I was going to have to have two seatings. Schuyler, Pritkin, Wilson, even Scott Raney, on Brandon's side; Tony Haselhorst, Brian, and not discounting Kevin Brody on Robbie's side, although Kevin was the one who'd hired me in the first place. And the mysterious man from New Orleans, Dennis Pine. About the only one I had eliminated was poor Raymond Sheed, and he only because no one would have been stupid enough to rent a murder car with his own credit card. And I didn't know how long I'd be allowed to operate before Ivy League Sergeant Ted Lawton pulled the plug on me.

I felt lousy, and the few bites of green shrimp I had eaten were paying return visits. I had a stiff neck, the beginnings of a headache, and I wasn't any closer to knowing anything than when Kevin Brody had sat himself down in my office and crossed his long, slim legs.

I stopped at my favorite liquor store about two blocks from my apartment and went inside past the displays of Inglenook wine and the *Playboy*s and *Penthouse*s and *Hustler*s the government hadn't been able to scare the proprietor out of carrying. The clerk recognized me and gave me a "Hello, Mr. Saxon," and I wondered if being recognized by a liquor store clerk wasn't a sign I was drinking too much.

"Running low on Laphroaig?" he said, bending down to a low shelf to where he kept the more obscure Scotches.

"Not tonight, Harry. Just—a gallon of chocolate ice cream."

14

"I don't believe what I'm hearing," Bill Laven said.

"Bill, I'm in the middle of a lot of things here and I don't have time to get into a philosophical discussion. Do you know of a school or not?" I took a bite of my toast and washed it down with my third cup of coffee of the morning. I was straining to hear over the sounds of "Take the A Train," which Marvel was playing for the third time that morning. I was very pleased that he was developing an appreciation for Duke Ellington, but at eight-thirty A.M. it was a little hard even for me to take. I held the phone between ear and shoulder as I reached for something to write with.

Bill said, "You might try the Bishop School in Westwood. But before you jump off the bridge don't you think you should check into the legal ramifications of this? I mean, are you going to adopt the boy? Become his legal guardian? Have you checked with the welfare people?"

"I haven't had time," I admitted.

"If I were you I'd make some," he said.

"I'll talk to George Ryon about it," I said. George was my attorney.

"George Ryon doesn't know about schools, he only knows about maximum-security prisons. Why don't I call my lawyer for you?"

"I'd really appreciate that, Bill. In the meantime I'll call the people at Bishop."

"When are we going to go to a ball game?"

"As soon as I can get out from under this case."

"The Cubs are in town weekend after next."

"Great! Make it the Sunday game?"

"You're on. I'll get the tickets."

"And Bill—get three tickets, will you?"

He sighed. "I swear to God, sometimes I think you need a keeper."

I hung up and walked out into the living room. The notes of a Harry Carney solo were bouncing off the walls like Ping-Pong balls, and Marvel was sitting in front of one of the speakers grooving on it. He looked up at me and said, "Tha's bad!"

"It sure is," I said. "It's also loud. Can you turn it down a little? I've got to make a long-distance call."

He got up and moved to the stereo as if he were going to his death, heaved a big martyred sigh, and turned the volume down. A little.

"More," I said.

"Man . . ." he said, and turned it down some more. Teen-agers the world over share being put upon by authority. I guess it was a good sign.

"Thanks, pal," I said, and went back into the bedroom.

I dialed New Orleans information and got the number of Ours, which, from its address, seemed to be in the French Quarter. Shades of Blanche DuBois.

"I'd like to speak to Dennis Pine, please," I said to the man who answered.

"Dennis isn't in this morning. He's out buying fabrics. May I take a message?"

"My name is James Ullman," I said, "with the Atlas Insurance Company here in Los Angeles."

"Oooh, all the way from Hollywood!" the man said. There was some sarcasm in the comment.

"Mr. Pine was witness to an automobile accident here in Los Angeles on June the thirteenth. I was hoping I could get a statement from him so we can go ahead and settle the claim."

There was a definite stage wait. "I think you have some wrong information, Mr. Ullman," he said. "And the wrong party."

"What do you mean?"

"Dennis hasn't been in Los Angeles for years."

"Are you sure of that?"

"We're roommates as well as co-owners of this shop. Dennis was here in New Orleans on June thirteenth. I'm as sure as I can possibly be."

"I see," I said, trying to sound puzzled. "Well, I don't know how his name got into our computers."

"That's the answer," he said. "Computers. They fuck up everything. Probably Dennis had a policy with you people a hundred years ago and somehow his name got onto the wrong diskette or something."

"Well, they're a necessary part of doing business these days, heh-heh," I said. "You're sure Mr. Pine was in New Orleans that morning?"

"Absolutely. Shall I have him call you when he comes back?"

"That's not necessary if I have the wrong party," I said. "And to whom am I speaking?"

"I'm Oliver van Rensselear," he said.

Sure you are. "Well, thank you very much, Mr. van Rensselear. I'm going to go push buttons and see how this mistake could have happened. You have a nice day, now."

"You, too," he said.

Unless his lover was covering for him, which seemed unlikely, I could cross Dennis Pine off my suspect list. It had been a long shot at best. Just to be sure, I called the office and left a message on the answering machine asking Jo to check the airlines and find out if a Dennis Pine had traveled between New Orleans and Los Angeles any time near June 13. I was pretty sure she'd come up empty, but there was no harm in being thorough.

Then I called the Bishop School and talked to a lady named Paula who had a very nice voice, and to whom I attempted to explain Marvel, leaving out where I'd found him and what he'd been doing up until a few days before.

"We ought to do some basic testing," she said. "Can you bring him in tomorrow?"

I thought of the Brandon case and how I seemed to be getting nowhere rapidly. I said, "Can we make it next week some time?"

"How about Wednesday?" she said. "Nine o'clock in the morning?"

"Wednesday sounds good." I made a notation on the message pad in the bedroom. I'd transfer it to my datebooks in the kitchen and at the office later.

"And how old did you say the boy was?"

I swallowed hard. "I—don't know."

"You don't know? Have you asked him?"

"Yes," I said. "He doesn't know, either."

I couldn't tell whether the sound she made was a chuckle or a *tsk* of disgust. But then she said, "This is beginning to interest me, Mr. Saxon."

"I'm glad," I told her.

I got myself some more coffee and sat down on the sofa. The music was back to blasting again, but at least I didn't have to watch cartoons.

"Marvel," I said.

"Yo."

"Marvel, where did you live before you came to Los Angeles?"

"Georgia," he said.

"Where in Georgia?"

He shrugged.

"Big city? Like Los Angeles? I mean, was it Atlanta?"

"Naw," he said. He tried to remember. "Not like 'Sangelus."

"Do you have a family?"

"You mean my momma? Yeah."

"Does she know where you are, Marvel?"

"Naw. She don' care, neither."

"Oh, I'm sure she does." I wasn't sure at all. "What's your last name?"

He just stared at me.

"Marvel what?"

"Um . . . Watkins."

"Marvel Watkins? And what was your mother's name?"

"Watkins too."

"I mean her first name?"

He thought a minute. "Lucille," he said.

"Did you go to school in Georgia?"

"Some. Then Leroy, he say I have to quit and work on the farm."

"When was this?"

"Long time ago."

"Who's Leroy? Your brother?"

He gave me a withering look, unable to comprehend the stupidity of anyone who didn't know who Leroy was. I imagined he was Lucille's boyfriend. Then Marvel said, "Leroy, he tol' me to git."

"He threw you out of the house?"

"Yo."

"And then what?"

"I took some money and I git."

"You stole some money from your momma?"

"Naw. From Leroy. An' I thumb a ride with this cat."

"What cat?"

"This cat, he say he goin' to—um, A'zona."

"Arizona?"

"Yeah. But then he make me do stuff with him."

"What stuff?"

"You know."

"He made you have sex with him?"

Marvel dropped his eyes.

"And did he take you to Arizona?"

"Yeah. But then he put me out the car. He take all Leroy's money, too."

"How did you get here?"

"Bus."

"Where'd you get the money?"

"I do more stuff."

"Where did you meet Tony?"

"He at the bus station. He say, 'You got a place to stay?' I say, 'Uh-uh.' He say, 'You wanta come with me?' I say, 'Yeah.' Then he tell me if'n I wants to live there I got to do stuff on the street and give him the money."

"You lived in Tony's apartment with him?"

"Uh-uh. Some other place. With other guys."

"Where? What was the address?"

"I dunno."

"Could you find it? Show me where it is?"

"I dunno. Kin I have mo' brekfuss?"

I waved a hand at the kitchen. "Help yourself." He went in and poured himself some more cereal and ate it standing up at the counter. I wondered how some people seemed to get all the good cards and some people didn't even get a chance to play.

"I'm going to my office, Marvel," I said. "I'll be home for dinner. Maybe we'll go out and grab a pizza." I picked up my keys. "Not this Sunday, but next Sunday we're going to a baseball game. You ever been to a ball game?"

"Jus' TV."

"Okay," I said. "We'll go see the Dodgers."

"Awri," he said.

It was one of those glorious California mornings when the smog had burned off early, and since I was heading eastward

I put the top down to work on my suntan. We in Southern California have an obligation to walk around looking like bronzed gods and goddesses so the rest of the country can hate us and say the sun has baked our brains and drained our ambition. I didn't care. Not long ago I'd sat in an outdoor café waiting for my lunch date, reading the newspaper accounts about blizzards in the Midwest that were killing cattle and blocking the roads while I was in my shirt sleeves. It was three days after Thanksgiving. I had endured enough Chicago winters, I'd figured. Now it was my turn.

I pulled into the lot behind my office on Ivar Avenue, half a block north of Hollywood Boulevard. It was a miserable neighborhood, but it was centrally located, and I had found over the years that more people in Hollywood needed a private detective than did those in Bel Air or Malibu. I simply ignored the teenage transvestites and the winos and the punkers and heavy-metal boys and the tourists from Iowa with eyes downcast looking for Tom Cruise's star on the Hollywood Walk of Fame. It was a place to work.

I didn't lock my car, since the top was down, and even if it had been up I preferred that anyone who wanted to get inside simply open the door, rather than slashing through the rag top. Out of the corner of my eye I saw three men get out of an Oldsmobile parked nearby and come toward me, and since I was in a business that occasionally could get sticky, I turned to face them.

The sun was in my eyes and at their backs, but I would have recognized the bulk of Barry Haworth anywhere. He was wearing a maroon sweat suit and resembled nothing more than a gigantic hairy plum. When they got closer I saw the two smaller men were Jimmy and Brian.

"Good morning," I said.

"We want to talk to you," Barry said in that high-pitched voice that never failed to surprise me.

171

"Okay. Come on up to the office."

"We'd like you to come with us," he said.

"Where to?"

"Someplace we can talk."

"We can talk upstairs."

A snub-nosed pistol appeared in Brian's hand. "Get in the car," he said, motioning toward the Olds.

"What is this?"

"Please don't make it any harder," Barry said.

"Well, we wouldn't want to make it harder. Do I put my hands up, or simply clasp them behind my head?"

"Move," Brian said, and he jammed the gun into my ribs with just a bit more force than I thought necessary.

It was a two-door model, and I was in the back seat on the left behind the driver, who was Barry. Brian sat in front with him, the gun trained on me but well out of my reach. Jimmy, who looked as disinterested as a passenger on a bus, was my seatmate. They turned north on Ivar, east on Yucca Street, and then off onto a little side street that wound up into the scrubby hills above Hollywood. After a while the houses started thinning out, then they disappeared altogether and the street became a two-lane blacktop road that seemed to head nowhere but up, a winding monotony. Finally I said, "Do I get clued in sometime, or is this a surprise."

"Shut up," Brian said.

"Shut up," Barry piped.

Jimmy didn't say anything, but I took his silence to be a concurrence with the majority. I shut up.

We stopped about a mile from the huge dam that hulks over Hollywood and got out and walked through the brittle grass for about a quarter of a mile, cockleburs sticking to our pants legs. We climbed down into a ditch that had been dug as a runoff for the winter rains, which otherwise would have buried Hollywood under tons of mud, and stopped. We were not visible from the road, or from anywhere else except straight up.

"Tony Haselhorst is very angry with you," Barry told me. "He's out on bail, and he's very angry."

"What's he got to do with you?" I said. Barry shot a quick glance at Jimmy and the look in his eyes was positively loving. Then he turned back to me. I said, "You mean you're doing Haselhorst's dirty work for him for a free piece of ass? Jesus, Barry!"

He slapped me across the face, hard, with the back of his hand. His weight behind it staggered me. "I don't expect you to understand," he said.

I tasted blood on my lower lip.

"I love Jimmy," he said. "This is the only way Tony will let me have him."

"For how long?" I said. "Or is he a keeper?"

Barry sighed. "Hold his arms, Jimmy."

Jimmy moved more quickly than I'd ever seen him, pinioning my arms behind me. He was strong for a little guy, but I think I could have broken the hold had it not been for Brian standing a few feet away, pointing the gun at my middle. Before I could get my bearings Barry stepped forward and punched me in the stomach as hard as he could. The breath rushed out of my lungs and I doubled over. My breakfast was at the back of my throat.

Barry grabbed a handful of my hair and pulled my head up. I noticed that somewhere along the way he had slipped a leather glove onto his right hand. "I want you to know," he said, "that there's nothing personal as far as I'm concerned."

And as the gloved fist came hurtling toward my face I reflected that it was small comfort.

∘ 15 ∘

It was somewhere after noon when I finally opened my eyes—and I use the term loosely, because they were both swollen almost shut. My head ached. My ribs and kidneys ached. My face hurt. One of my teeth was loose, but it was on the side and I didn't worry too much about it. My main concern was for my nose, but while I was still sitting in the drainage ditch I worked it around with my fingers and ascertained that it was not broken. As many times as I have been hit in the face no one has ever managed to break my nose. For that I was grateful. My nose is somewhat prominent, but it's straight, and if it were ever to get broken it would probably never be the same. Maybe I was in the wrong business.

I had no memory of Barry and his two friends leaving. He'd kept on hitting me until I passed out, and then I suppose they took off. It was an amateurish job; a professional knows all too well how to make a beating last a long time. I was lucky Tony Haselhorst had been too penurious to hire professional muscle and had sent three minor leaguers to do the job for him.

I staggered back to the road, my bruised ribs protesting every step. It was highly unlikely that a taxi was going to come cruising by up here where the only inhabitants were hawks and rabbits and coyotes, so I began trudging back along the side of the road. I was thankful it was downhill all the way. By the time I had reached the first house I'd decided no one was going to let a bloodied stranger in to make a phone call, but after another ten minutes I elected to chance it and stopped at one of the houses that perched on stilts over the edge of the canyon.

The man who opened the door was elderly and grizzled

and wore gray work pants and a plaid shirt. The red skin on his chest was bumpy, like a turkey's. "Oh, my!" he said through the screen.

"I'm sorry to bother you," I said, "but I need to make a call. If you don't want to let me in I'll understand, but maybe you could make the call for me. I have identification—"

"Hell, come on in," he said, unhooking the screen door and opening it wide. "You don't look in any shape to give anyone trouble."

"Thank you," I grunted, and went past him into the house. It was untidy without being really messy and smelled of last night's chili. I guessed the man lived alone, as there was no evidence of a woman's touch anywhere in the cluttered living room.

"You have a car accident?" he said.

"Yes. I need to call my office."

"Where's that ID you spoke of?"

I took out my wallet and showed him my driver's license. He studied it carefully, trying to match the stiffly smiling face in the picture with the somewhat misshapen one that confronted him. Then he handed it back.

"You look like you could use a drink," he said. "All I've got is bourbon."

"That's fine," I said. I hated bourbon, but at the moment it sounded wonderful. He took a bottle of cheap booze and poured three fingers of it into a green plastic tumbler and handed it to me.

"Got no ice," he said.

"Don't want any," I said. I took a gulp of the whiskey and almost hit the ceiling when the alcohol passed over my bleeding lip. It reached my stomach and lay there like battery acid.

"Phone's in the kitchen," he said. I nodded and followed his pointing finger into a tiny kitchen. Washed dishes stood in a rubber drainer on the counter. The phone was a wall model, faded yellow, with a dial instead of push buttons. It took me one false start before my shaking fingers were able to dial the correct seven digits.

"Saxon Investigations," Jo sang.

"Jo, I've had a little trouble," I said.

"Oh my God!" she wailed. "What's the matter?"

The Jewish mother in Jo surfaces in times of crisis. I'd seen it before.

"I'll explain when I see you," I said. "Can you lock up the office and come get me. I'm at. . . ?" I looked at the old man, who was standing at the entrance to the kitchen watching me.

He said, "Twenty-seven seventy-four Durfee Canyon Road."

I repeated the address to her and gave her general directions.

"Do you need a doctor?" Her voice quavered.

"I don't know yet," I said. "We'll talk about it when I see you."

"Ten minutes," she said, and hung up. I did the same, and turned back to the old man. "Someone will be here for me in about ten minutes. Is there someplace I could sit down?"

"Sofa," he said. I followed him back into the living room and sank gratefully down onto the sagging sofa with the faded floral covers. I leaned my head back and closed my eyes, feeling pretty shaky. Somehow the plastic glass in my hand gave me a more secure feeling, something to hang on to.

After a few moments my host said quietly, "You're a pretty poor liar, son." I opened my eyes. He was looking at me not unkindly. "You didn't have no accident at all. You was beaten up."

I didn't say anything. He hadn't put it as a question.

"My name's Paul Stanoyevich, but most everyone calls me Slim. Spent a lotta years as a longshoreman, so I recognize the marks of a beating. What with union problems and one thing and another I've been worked over a time or two. And I've been on the delivery end. You know the guys who done this to you?"

I nodded.

"You deserve it?"

"I can't answer that. It depends on where you're standing."

"See what you mean. Drink up, there's more."

I finished my drink and he refilled the tumbler.

"I really appreciate this, Slim," I said.

"Hell, you can't reach out your hand to a fellow human being, you're not worth rat shit. You feel like talking about your troubles?"

"I can't," I said. "It's very complicated. I'm a private investigator and I'm working on a case."

"Hah! Sounds like you rattled somebody's chain."

"Something like that."

"He do it himself, or send someone?"

"Sent three someones."

Slim waved his hand in a gesture of dismissal. "That's the sign of a scared man," he said. "You must have the goods on him."

"No," I said. "If he had something to hide he'd be hiding it, not having me beaten up by guys who told me where it was coming from."

He scratched his stubbly jawline and nodded. "You got a point, there," he said. "You think like a detective."

"Damn good thing," I said.

"How'd you ever get into that line of work?"

I put my head back again but kept my eyes open. "I came to Los Angeles to be an actor. I did okay, but I finally got tired of living from job to job. I tried punching a time clock, but I'm not very good at that."

"Independent cuss, eh?"

"Yeah. So I needed to start my own business, one where I

could keep my own hours, and if an acting job came along I could take it and not worry. So here I am."

I heard a car out in front, and then the engine was cut off, a door slammed, and Jo Zeidler appeared at the screen in silhouette, peering through the mesh with one hand shading her pretty eyes.

"Come in, darlin'," Slim said, ushering her in. He looked at her with appreciation. "Those movies are true; you private cops always have the prettiest girls."

I didn't bother correcting him. Jo came and looked down at me, biting the inside of her cheek. I waited for her words of sympathy, balm for my aching body.

"You're a mess," she said.

I was lying on the couch in my office with a bag of ice on my face and another one on my ribs under the heart. I didn't feel very well, but my mind was working overtime.

Jo was sitting behind my desk, making notes as I spoke. For all Jo's emotionalism she was a terrific assistant and had often functioned as a sounding board. I had decided to spool some of my theories out for her and see what she thought.

"Tony Haselhorst had every right to be pissed off at me," I said. "I not only stole his star performer right out from under his nose, but I slapped him around—twice—and then called the law on him. My only mistake was in underestimating him. I thought he'd be too chickenshit to retaliate. He wasn't. His tough-guy reputation on the boulevard had to be protected, because if I can come in and fuck him over then pretty soon everybody's doing it and he's out of business."

"Doesn't it follow, then, that if Haselhorst wanted Robbie to work for him and couldn't get him that he'd take the same kind of retaliation?" Jo said.

"Exactly my point. He would have taken the same kind of retaliation—had Robbie beaten up, maybe messed up his face so he wasn't so pretty or so saleable anymore. He wouldn't have killed him. And if he had, he would've bragged about it."

"You're pretty sure?"

I nodded, which caused little starbursts of pain to go off behind my eyes. "I've known enough pimps in my day, straight or otherwise. They're ninety percent ego. Look at the way they strut around the streets in velvet jumpsuits and big beaver hats and customized pimp-mobiles. They keep their status by intimidation, by polishing their reputation. They punish someone as an object lesson, they're going to advertise it. That's why Tony wouldn't have killed Robbie—at least, not that way. He would've had him beaten to death or cut up and left on the street on Santa Monica Boulevard, and everyone in that world would've known within twenty-four hours that Tough Tony Haselhorst had punished someone who had defied him and that's what was waiting for the next guy who tried it. Uh-uh. Tony is scum, and he may have wanted to kill me when I hassled him yesterday, but that was blind anger. He could very easily have had those three guys finish me off this morning, but he didn't. And I don't think he killed Robbie Bingham."

"Who did?"

"That's the burning question. But I'll bet anything that the primary target of the hit was Steven Brandon."

"You're eliminating Kevin Brody as a suspect? After he admitted he was cheating with that Brian?"

"Joanne, lots of husbands and or wives cheat. You and Marsh are just about the only couple I know that doesn't."

"Don't be too sure," she said, her eyes twinkling. It was all talk. She'd never cheat on Marsh Zeidler. It would be like mugging an old lady.

"You've got to remember something. Ask almost anyone to define themselves in one word and they'd be hard put for an answer. What would you say: career woman, wife, Jewish lady, bookkeeper? How about me? Actor, detective, gourmet? There are a lot of things that most people could say about themselves, and they wouldn't know which one to choose. Ah, but homosexuals are another story. Most of them would define themselves in terms of their own gayness. First and foremost they are homosexuals—*then* they are artists or salesmen or tennis players or Zen Buddhists or whatever else happens to be going on in their lives. And as such they are extremely sexual people."

"I have a boss like that," she said.

I ignored the sarcasm. "It only stands to reason that, no matter how much he loved Robbie, if their sex life was at a low ebb Kevin would go elsewhere for satisfaction. It was a temporary thing, I'm sure, but hardly a reason for murder. Besides, why would Kevin have hired me to find the killer in the first place if I might discover it was him?"

"To throw suspicion elsewhere?"

"You've been reading too many bad detective novels and not enough Raymond Chandler," I said.

"It's possible."

"Possible, but not very probable. Kevin's grief was genuine enough. Besides, he told me himself he was messing around with Brian."

"So where does that leave us?"

"As far as I'm concerned, it narrows it down to someone who wanted Brandon dead."

We both heard the door to the outer office open and close. Jo stood up. "I'll get rid of whoever it is," she said. "You're in no shape for company."

I strained to hear what was going on in the reception room. I could make out two feminine voices, but not what they were saying. With any luck it was a Girl Scout selling cookies and I wouldn't have to talk to her.

Jo came back in, shutting the door behind her. "It's a Jennifer London. I told her you couldn't see anyone, but she's being insistent."

I moved my head very carefully so as not to set off the shooting stars again. "I might as well see her," I said.

Jo put her hand on the doorknob, smirked at me, and silently mouthed "Bimbo" before going out.

A few seconds later Jennifer appeared, wearing a pair of fawn-colored slacks and a red blouse, and it might be said without contradiction that she was a sight for sore eyes. Very sore eyes.

"My God," she said, a hand to her mouth, "what happened?"

"I had some trouble."

She chewed on the knuckle of her index finger but made no move to come to me. "Who did it?"

"Doesn't matter. What are you doing here, Jennifer?"

"I was afraid you were mad at me," she said in a little-girl voice. "I came to make it okay."

"I'm not mad at you."

"You sure?"

"Jennifer, I'm in a lot of pain right now—"

"Oh, I know, I wouldn't have come if . . . I really like you and I didn't want you to give up on me."

She came and sat next to me on the sofa, but not too close. She seemed fascinated that a relatively pleasant face could have been transformed almost overnight into the Elephant Man. She couldn't quite help drawing her upper lip back in disgust. Her teeth were very white and straight. "Was it the killer who beat you up?"

"No," I said, putting my elbows on my knees and lowering my head to fight off the waves of dizziness. "The guys who did this are Robbie Bingham's friends, and the intended victim of that bomb was Steven Brandon, so the two incidents are unrelated. Now be a good girl and run along so you don't have to see me whimper."

"Will you call me tonight?"

"No, I won't call you tonight. I'm going to go home and sleep this off. I'll call you when I'm up and around again. Okay?"

She stood up, her eyes narrowing. "Typical male," she said. "You expect a woman to just sit by the phone until you feel like calling." Her shoulders heaved with resignation. "All right, then," she said, and went out, through the reception room and past Jo, who looked at her as though she were Typhoid Mary.

I called my client in Malibu, who didn't seem terribly anxious to talk to me. Finally he said, "Saxon, I'm goddamn embarrassed about what I told you—about Dennis Pine. I really feel like an idiot."

"Mr. Brandon," I said, "I was beaten up this morning and I don't have time for your head games. I still don't know who was behind it, but I'm relatively convinced that bomb was meant for you."

He was silent for a moment. Softly, almost in a whisper, "Was it Dennis?"

"No," I said. "He hasn't been out of New Orleans in years. And I didn't talk to him, and I didn't mention your name or even my name, so everything is cool. What I'm calling you about is this: I'd like to send a friend of mine out to stay with you for a couple of days. His name is Ray Tucek and I think you'll enjoy his company."

"You're going to send me company, make it a lady, will you?"

"Fine idea, but I don't know any ladies who fought heavyweight in the Golden Gloves and had three years of hand-to-hand combat in Southeast Asia. I'd really feel better if Ray were there."

"You think it's that bad?"

"I'd feel better and I'd think you would, too."

He thought about it. "Okay," he said.

"Don't you want to know what it's going to cost you?"

"No," he said.

I called my friend Ray Tucek, a card-carrying member of the Stuntman's Association who often helped me out when I thought a bodyguard was in order. Ray is a gentle soul with a taste for Scotch and a body that makes Sylvester Stallone look like Don Knotts. He is frighteningly good with a pistol and handles a hunting knife the way Rod Carew used to handle a bat: with deadly accuracy and control. Easygoing most of the time, Ray Tucek's wrath when finally aroused is awesome to behold and nearly impossible to withstand. In addition, he has the loyalty of a sheepdog, a quick and inquiring mind, and a sense of humor that is often as snide and cutting as my own. He is a good guy to know, to drink with, and to have on your side. And although he makes a pretty good living when he works in films, he is always in need of money.

"Why can't you ever get me a gig guarding a body like Jaclyn Smith's?" he said.

"Stop whining. You go out to Malibu with your toothbrush and your jammies, you spend a few days soaking up rays on the sun deck, you watch the teenage beach bunnies frolic in the surf, and there seems to be a limitless supply of beer and booze—and, oh yes, I forgot to mention Inger."

"Inger?" I could hear the interest in his voice. "Who's Inger?"

"She's Swedish," I said cryptically.

"I love Swedes."

"Then you're in luck."

He asked me how much the job paid. I thought of Brandon saying he didn't care how much more a bodyguard would cost him, and I upped Ray's usual price by twenty-five dollars a day. Brandon would either write it off his income taxes or figure out a way to get the network to pay for it.

After I talked to Ray I called the nearby liquor store and asked them to deliver six bottles of Jack Daniels to Slim Stanoyevich up on Durfee Canyon Road. I was a firm believer that if enough good deeds went unrewarded, pretty soon people would stop doing them.

○ **16** ○

When I finally walked in the door of my place that eve-ning, I thought Marvel was going to cry when he saw my face. He didn't ask any questions for a long while. He just said, "Man!" and led me to the sofa. He eased me down onto it and without my asking he went into the kitchen and found two clean dish towels, filled them with ice cubes, and brought them out to me. Then he went into the back bathroom and got some Tylenol and a glass of water. He brought a pillow from the bedroom and gently slid it under my head.

"Better?" he said. His unlined face showed a lot of concern.

"Yeah. Thanks, pal. That's a lot better."

"You want some booze?"

I had to consider that for a while, but I finally decided it would make me feel worse and shook my head. He turned off the TV and most of the lights in the room, leaving one lamp on near the window. Then he pulled a dining room chair out and sat down right next to me, his elbows on his knees, his chin resting in his two cupped hands.

"Marvel, I'll be okay. Really."

"I know it," he said. "You ain' been whupped bad."

"Bad enough."

"Shee-it," he said. "Tony beat on us this bad every couple days. You be okay—keep that ice on you' nose, now, fool."

I did what he said, and after a few minutes I dropped off into a troubled, shallow sleep, coming awake with a myo-clonic jerk every few minutes. Each time I opened my eyes, he was there. Finally I said, "Marvel, I think I'd like to take a shower and wash the blood off."

"Take a bath," he said. "Relax you'self." And when I started to sit up he said, "I do it," and went into the bathroom and ran me a hot, steamy bath. I yelled in to him that there were epsom salts under the sink and to put some in the water, and I guess he did it because a few minutes later when the tub was full and he helped me ease myself into it I immediately felt some of the soreness being drawn out of my body. He even rolled up a bath towel and put it behind my head so I could unwind completely, and he sat on the edge of the closed toilet to keep me company. After a few minutes he took a washcloth and gently wiped the remaining dried blood off my face, being very careful of my split lip. He examined it carefully. "Not too bad," he pronounced with all the confidence of a second-year resident. "It be okay."

When the bathwater began to cool he came over and ran some more hot until the water level reached the edge of the tub, then turned it off and sat back down.

"Who do this?" he said.

"Some guys."

"Tony?"

I debated lying to him and decided against it. "He had it done."

His eyes filled with tears. "Cuz o' me."

"No, Marvel, not because of you."

"For real?"

"For real. I'll tell you all about it when I'm feeling better. It had nothing to do with you."

"Tha's good," he said. There was relief on his face.

After about ten more minutes my fingers were wrinkled and pink, and a lot of the pain had left my body via the hot water. I decided it was time to get out. Marvel helped me to stand up and handed me a towel, and when I was dry he was right there with my bathrobe. It was nice to be fussed over, feeling the way I did, and I didn't argue.

I started for the living room but he put a hand firmly at the small of my back and began steering me toward my bed. "I sleep out there," he said.

"It's okay."

"Uh-uh, it ain't." He was going to brook no discussion, so I allowed him to guide me to the bed. I lay down gingerly. After he made sure I was covered and switched off the light he stopped in the doorway, silhouetted against the dim light from the living room. "Call me if you wan'," he said.

"Okay. Good night, Marvel."

"Night."

"And—thanks."

"Yeah," he said.

Within ninety seconds I was asleep.

I awoke shortly after seven o'clock the next morning, and already I could hear the muffled sounds of the TV from the next room. It had probably been watched more in the last few days than in the past year, as I generally restrict my TV watching to baseball, the news, and an occasional old movie. When I tried to sit up the memory of the morning before was reinforced by the introduction of a headache that would have stopped a charging rhinoceros. I sank back down and the throbbing subsided somewhat, but not enough to make me feel good. I was having a certain amount of trouble breathing through my nose, and my lip felt like someone else's lip had been grafted onto it. It was definitely what would, under ordinary circumstances, be a stay-in-bed day, but I had things to do.

When I staggered out into the living room the sunlight filtering through the open drapes struck me in the face like a Nolan Ryan hummer, and I groaned audibly. Marvel was immediately on his feet and at my side, all concern. I threw my arm around his shoulder in a rather forced display of bonhomie. "Usually when I feel like this in the morning it means I had a good time last night," I said.

"Take it easy," he said.

I navigated slowly into the kitchen and poured myself a

glass of orange juice. "Marvel, be a good guy and bring me three Tylenol, would you?" I said. I took a swallow of the orange juice and struggled manfully to keep it where it was supposed to be.

Later, in the bathroom, I surveyed the damage to my face. It wasn't too bad. My nose was still swollen, but at least it looked as though it belonged on a human being. A scab had crusted over my lower lip, and there were discolorations around both eyes that promised to turn into rather impressive shiners within the next twenty-four hours. The bones beneath the skin were sore and tender, and I shaved with great care, avoiding the spot below the gash in my lip. By the time I had dressed and put on a pair of sunglasses, an affectation I normally eschewed, I looked almost alive. I didn't feel that way, though, as the Tylenol had made hardly a dent in my headache.

"Best you stay in bed," Marvel said when he saw I was dressed to go out.

"You're right," I said. "But I've got things to do."

"I make you some toast."

While he was fussing in the kitchen I called Jo at home to tell her I was all right. She sounded tired.

"Rough night?" I said.

"Probably not as rough as yours."

"Want to talk about it?"

"Marsh was really upset when he heard what happened to you. He thinks I should be in a safer line of work."

"He's right. What do you think?"

After a pause, she said, "I'll see you at the office."

I was more than relieved. I didn't know what I would do without Jo. I didn't know what her husband would do without her, either. Marsh Zeidler was one of those people who tiptoed through life picking up the crumbs other people had left him, and without Jo's encouragement about his truly rotten screenwriting he would probably be living in one room someplace, waiting on tables in Westwood as he now did and kvetching that no one would give him a break.

Marvel had not only made toast but a fairly decent pot of coffee, grinding the beans in my little electric grinder as I'd showed him. While I ate, he sat opposite me at the table shaking his head and telling me I shouldn't go out today.

"Listen, Marvel," I said, "pretty soon the pressure is going to ease up and things will get to normal around here. I'll be home more, and we can kind of get to know each other."

"I just be mo' trouble," he said.

"Probably," I said. "But you've got a lot to bring to the party, too. I really appreciate the way you took care of me last night. I couldn't have made it through without you, and that's the truth."

"Tha's okay," Marvel said. He poured me some more coffee, and before I had finished it the doorbell rang.

Now, there are many people who might be begging entrance to your home at nine o'clock on a Friday morning who wouldn't particularly surprise you. It might be the landlord come to check out the complaints of the guy downstairs that there was a leak under your kitchen sink. It could be one of those kids who tell you that if you buy an overpriced box of his crappy peanut brittle he'll win a trip to summer camp. It could be the hapless bachelor-accountant from across the hall wanting to borrow your nutmeg or your blender or your *TV Guide*. It could be, but all too frequently is not, an ex-lover feeling restless and bored who just dropped by for some comfort. Perhaps it's a term life insurance drummer who just happened to be in the building and thought he'd stop by to talk to you about building an estate. None of these dropping by and punching your doorbell would cause a raised eyebrow. One expects them, in a large city, with monotonous regularity.

But when your visitor is a man who, not twenty-four hours before, slipped a leather driving glove over his fist and whaled the kapok out of you while another man held you and a third pointed a gun at you, the visit is, to say the least, unexpected. It doesn't exactly set your heart to singing, either.

Barry Haworth was standing far back from the door, probably so that I couldn't reach him with one good swing. He was wearing his gray sweats and a pair of tinted glasses, and he looked like a giant Smurf.

"I know you're mad at me," he said.

I couldn't help laughing. "*Mad* at you? You son of a bitch, I'd like to tear your face off, and I would if I didn't ache in every bone. What do you want?"

"I just came to see if you're all right."

"Now's a hell of a time to worry about that!"

He turned his hands palms up. "May I come in?"

"I'll say this for you. You've got balls." I stood aside and he walked gingerly past me into the living room. I followed, closing the door. Marvel was standing near the TV, wide-eyed.

"Hello, Marvel," Barry said. It startled me for a moment until I realized that with Barry's deep involvement with Tony Haselhorst he would obviously know Marvel. Marvel just nodded at him. I noticed Marvel's hands were balled into fists, and I was flooded with a warm feeling. The kid was ready to mix it up with a man twice his size to protect me.

Barry sat down on the couch, on the edge, as if ready to fly at any moment. He said, "I want to apologize. I feel really lousy about yesterday and I wanted you to know. I promise you that you won't have any more trouble from Tony. I'll see to it."

I went and picked up my mug. "You want coffee?" I said. Ever the gracious host. I couldn't believe I was doing this.

"No," he said. "You have every right to take a swing at me, and if you want to, go ahead. I don't blame you."

"If I take a swing at you," I said, "it's not going to be where I'll bust up my own furniture." There was a drum and bugle corps playing behind my eyes, minus the bugles. I brought my coffee mug to my lips with a shaky hand. "Why this sudden attack of conscience?"

"I don't know," he said. "I never did anything like that before. I've been in fights, sure, but I never beat up a man because someone else told me to. I'm not like that."

"Uh-huh." I looked over at Marvel. He seemed to have relaxed, but he still stood on the balls of his feet in case anything happened. It was comforting.

"It was emotional blackmail," he said. "I realize that now."

"Too bad you didn't realize it yesterday," I said, fingering my sore face.

"If I hadn't done it somebody else would have. And they might have hurt you a lot worse."

I nodded. I saw the logic in that.

"So I just came by to tell you I was sorry."

I stared at him for a long while, and then I began to laugh.

"What's funny?"

"This is the damnedest thing I ever heard of," I said. "I've been beaten up before, but this is my first formal apology for it."

"Do you accept it?"

"What if I don't?"

He shrugged his massive shoulders. "I'll feel even worse."

"We couldn't have that, Barry. All right, I accept your apology."

He sat back on the sofa, happy again. Then he sat forward once more and said, "Jimmy's sorry, too."

I didn't say anything.

"Have you ever been in love?" he said.

"Sure."

"So in love that you were obsessed by it, that all you could think about was that person? So that you did really stupid things, things you wouldn't have dreamed of before, just to be with that person?"

I sighed, remembrances of old pains fighting with the ache in my head for my attention.

"Well, that's the way I am with Jimmy," he went on. "I know what he is, I know he's not much to look at, but then neither am I. And I was willing to do anything just to be with him. Tony said that if I—did what he wanted, that he'd release Jimmy, let him stay with me. I can make something of that boy. He's got potential." He looked down at his pudgy fingers, which were moving as though he were molding clay. "My love for him made me lose my judgment yesterday, made me do a rotten thing. I'll never forgive myself for it."

"Did you get what you wanted?" I said. "Did Tony keep his word?"

Barry smiled like a huge child. "Jimmy moved in with me last night. With all his stuff."

"Well, at least something came out of it."

"But it wouldn't have been any good unless I came out here and said what I have to say," he said. "I had to take two buses to get here, too."

"Don't you have a car?"

He shook his head. "I'm a sculptor," he said. "I live in my studio, and I hardly ever have to leave the neighborhood, so I always figured it was an unnecessary expense."

"Listen, Barry. Since you're in such a mea culpa mood, maybe you can answer a couple of questions for me."

I could see his eyes grow wary behind the glasses.

"Was there any reason Tony had you guys mess me up other than pure revenge?"

"What other reason could he have?"

"Robbie Bingham," I said.

Barry scratched his head, and in the early morning sunlight I could see the dandruff flakes settling onto the back of my couch like a spring snowfall. "If you're trying to make Tony fit into the Bingham killing, I think you're wasting your time."

"Why?"

"Tony's capable of killing—in a blind rage, maybe. But to plan it out that way? To set up a remote-control explosion? Or time it out that way? Tony just doesn't have the intellectual capability. He is a mean and vicious son of a bitch—"

"For real!" Marvel chimed in earnestly.

"—but I don't think he's up to planning a careful murder."

I wandered into the kitchen and put my now empty coffee mug in the dishwasher, which was full of glasses stained with the residue of milk or soda, a most unusual sight in my apartment. I knew, of course, that Barry's saying it didn't make it so, but his assessment of Tony Haselhorst pretty much coincided with mine. Call it a gut instinct. I leaned my aching head against the coolness of the refrigerator for a moment and then went back to Barry and Marvel.

"I hate to bust up this meeting of the Breakfast Club," I said, "but this is a working day."

"You really ought to take the day off," Barry said. "You need time to recuperate."

"Your concern, under the circumstances, is touching," I said. "Marvel, you'll be okay?"

"Yo."

I struggled into my jacket, and Barry was on his feet to help, the Angel of the Death Camps soothing his victims even while the torture was increased. "And you're not mad at me anymore?" he said.

"Only when I laugh."

"Well, can I ask you a big favor? Can I get a lift with you into Hollywood, if it's not too much out of your way?"

"Of course," I said. "We're friends, aren't we?"

We went down to the subterranean garage, every jolt of the elevator making my head feel as though a demented soprano was inside screeching the mad scene from *Lucia*. Barry and Marvel were right—I should have stayed home in bed with cold compresses. I didn't know how I was going to make it through the day without massive doses of painkiller, but I had to go to the office, had to review the notes, to shift the pieces around on the table until somehow they fit together to give me a picture.

We got to the Fiat. "You drive," I said, handing my car keys to Barry.

He looked at them, then at the car dubiously. "It's been a long time since I've driven a stick."

"You'll do better than I could," I said. "With my headache I'd be lucky to see the road."

"Okay," he said, "but when I strip the gears don't yell."

"Yelling would make my head hurt," I said.

Fortunately the rag top was down, making it just a bit easier for Barry to maneuver his huge bulk behind the wheel and to adjust the seat backward to give him some breathing room. I left him and went over to the automatic gate that was no longer automatic, opened the control box and pushed the button, waited until the ponderous metal gate began its tortuous journey across the entrance, and started back to the car just in time to see Barry turn the key in the ignition. The entire front half of my car disappeared in a screaming fireball, and the force of the explosion knocked me flat on my back. It blew the hood, the grill, the windshield, scattered engine parts, and Barry Haworth all over the wall of the garage.

○ 17 ○

To see a man die is to take up permanent residence on that lonely, windswept rocky shore that is the spawning ground of the nightmare, to live side by side with those black-winged Furies that lurk in dark closets and in the shadows of night-time alleyways and behind the doors of musty attics with their smells of the long past and of futures filled with dread, to be of them, the children of the Pit, who tickle the base of your spine and crawl on the back of your neck during those predawn hours when sleep won't come and you don't want it to because it will bring along with it the childhood fears you manage to stuff down into your subconscious all day, as though the light of the sun might bring them hideously to life to fly at your face when you're eating your lunch or driving the freeway or taking in a ball game. But at night they refuse to remain where you've stored them. They come creeping out to look around and spread their slimy wings to dry and flick their lizard tongues at you and chortle at your pitiful efforts to keep them buried deep, where they belong. To watch a man die is to hand over your ticket of entry to Cerberus, guardian of the underworld, to be punched and validated— to watch a man die and know he is dying in your stead.

Finally the police left, and the coroner's men, and the fo-rensics experts and the bomb squad, and it was just my little happy circle of family remaining: Jo, whom I had called at the office and who had come rushing over, pausing to summon Ray Tucek from the sun-baked beach of Malibu because she felt I needed guarding more than did Steven Brandon; and Marvel, who more than any of them seemed to take a car-bombing in his stride. It might have been the worst thing he'd ever seen, but Marvel had witnessed a lot over on the dark side of the moon where he'd spent most of his young life, and a corpse that wasn't a corpse at all but only shattered pieces of bone and matter wouldn't make the same kind of impact on him as it would on most teenage boys.

Jo had been quite insistent about calling in a doctor to sedate me, but I had been adamant. I had to be awake, sharp, with as many of my faculties as were currently functional. The answer was there, but it couldn't seem to cut through my headache.

We had done every "poor Barry" we had in us for the moment. I had told the police as much as I knew about him, but I had no idea if he'd left a family, parents, siblings. Barry was one of those people who just seem to be, found in all the metropolitan centers of the world, who breathe and work and piss and sleep and then go away and the space they leave is immediately closed up, like digging a hole in soft sand, so that at their passing no one knows they've ever been there. I had no idea what was going to happen to Jimmy, or maybe I did, but there was no room at the inn as far as I was concerned. My own personal Dotheboys' Hall was sporting a No Vacancy sign.

Ray Tucek was working on my Scotch, and when he'd drunk enough of it to lubricate his tongue he said, "Well, sport, it looks like somebody's awful scared of you."

"Or hates my guts," I said.

"Naw. You hate a man, you do something mean to him. Wreck his career, ball his wife, poison his dog. When you set a bomb in his car it means you're scared of him."

"I'm just little," I said.

"But you know something."

"I don't know anything! That's what's bugging me."

"Sure you do. You must. Think about it."

"Ray, let him alone," Jo said mildly. "He needs to get some rest."

"He can't get any rest with a big old chicken bone in his throat," Ray said. "Let him cough it out and look at it. Then he'll rest." He grinned over at me. "Do I know my customers or what?"

"What," I answered. I went into the bathroom and splashed cold water on my face for the tenth time, shuddering, remembering the moment I had picked myself up from the garage floor and gone over to see what was left of my car and its driver. I looked at my dripping visage in the mirror, and then I started to cry. I was crying for Barry, I was crying for all the Barrys and Jimmys and Marvels in the world. And I was crying for me, too, for the understandable but not terribly noble relief I was feeling that I had asked Barry to drive and not turned that key in the ignition myself. I cried until I thought all the tears were out of me, and then I threw up into the toilet, and then I cried some more.

I was sitting on the floor, practically wedged between the side of the tub and the toilet bowl, the porcelain a source of cold comfort, and then there was a soft tapping at the door and Marvel stuck his head in.

"Come on," he said, and came all the way in. "Come on, git you to bed now." He helped me to stand up, quite a feat considering I outweighed him by fifty pounds, and he hugged me around the shoulders to let me know it was going to be all right, and for the second time in twenty-four hours he assisted me to the bed and made sure I was there for a while, and then he said, "It's okay. We be right outside."

And I slept. Fitfully. The nightmares were starting, and I knew there would be no peace, no rest for me until I had laid the ghost. It was times like these that a man needed a significant other, arms around him, someone to cry to who would hold him and stroke him and chase the demons from the bedchamber and replace them with soft, sweet flesh and hair that smelled of spring lilacs. And that activated a lot of the old pains again, trotted out to parade across the coverlet like a madhouse "March of the Wooden Soldiers."

And then I sat upright in bed, drenched in sweat, swallowing the scream that I might have let live had it been the dead of night. And I knew. The pieces finally fit.

18

I waited until it got dark. I didn't have to; it could as easily have been done in sunlight. But there are some scenes that play better in shadow, those dark deeds of the heart that seem to be a part of the night.

I listened at the door for a moment. Music was playing, an old Janis Ian album from a younger and more innocent time when we were all seventeen in our hearts. I rang the bell and heard murmurs under the music. Then the door was opened, the light inside spilling out into the subdued illumination of the hallway.

"Hello, Jennifer," I said.

As usual she wasn't wearing much makeup, so when the blood rushed from her face at the sight of me, leaving it pale and drawn, I could see the fine bones of her face. She put a hand up to her throat.

"Oh!" she said. She took a step backward. And then she made a conscious effort to get her act together. "Well, this is a surprise."

"I imagined it would be. Aren't you going to invite me in for a drink?"

She shot a quick, guilty glance over her shoulder. "Um, this really isn't such a great time. I was going to turn in early. I mean, if you'd called first—"

"That would have wrecked the surprise," I said. I brushed past her into the apartment, and the air was alive with cigarette smoke and perfume and perhaps the merest hint of a good *blanc de blancs*. A filter-tipped butt smoldered in the ashtray. "I won't take up too much of your time."

She stood there for a moment, nostrils flaring, unattractive white lines of stress at the corners of her lips. "Look," she said, "I know I said I wanted to see you again, but most of my dates usually call, like gentlemen."

"Do they? Like gentlemen?" I sat down on the sofa. "You seem really startled."

"I am. I mean, you never told me you were coming over. I would have cleaned up, put something nice on." She stubbed out the cigarette. "This just is not a good time."

"You've been so anxious about the bombing, asking me if I'd found out who did it. Well, I've found out and I wanted to share it with you. Lay all your foolish fears to rest."

She chewed on her lip. "Your face looks better," she said.

"Time heals all wounds. Don't you want to hear my news? Wait, I think we all should hear it."

Her forehead wrinkled in puzzlement. "What do you mean?"

"Don't you want to let your friend in on the fun?" I got up, strolled over to the bedroom door, and opened it. "Come on out, Sanda."

There was a moment, just a moment, when I thought I had blown it, as the bedroom was dark. Then I heard a rustling and Sanda Schuyler walked out past me. She was wearing a man's bathrobe over expensive-looking tailored silk pajamas.

"Nice to see you again, Sanda," I said.

"What is this all about, Mr. Saxon? How dare you barge your way in here? There are laws—"

"Indeed there are. Too many, I think sometimes. I for one always drive too fast on the freeways. But there are some laws we need—the ones about murder, for instance."

"What are you babbling about?"

"Murder. Homicide. You remember: another of those male-dominated fields. You had me going for a while. Both of you."

"I think you'd better go," Sanda said.

"I think you'd better listen. You might learn something."

"From you?" She lit up another cigarette and blew the smoke in my face. It was not only the ultimate put-down, but to do it to someone who's just quit the habit was downright cruel. I waved the smoke away.

"It was the perfect setup," I said. "Only one witness—Jennifer, who had no connection with Robbie Bingham or Steven Brandon—to give a nice, neat, yet vague description of the man who rented the murder car. I liked especially the part where Jennifer said he was sort of strange, that he didn't flirt with her. That would send the police looking for someone in the gay community, someone who killed Robbie Bingham, with poor Steven Brandon an unfortunate second victim. Where did you get the mustache, Sanda? Did you swipe it from the network's makeup department or just go out and buy it at a theatrical makeup store?"

She didn't answer. Neither of them did. Sanda's face was a mask, her eyes dead and cold. Jennifer was just staring at her, terrified.

"I'm sure the suit is one of yours. You wear man-tailored suits a lot, don't you? Of course, usually with a nice feminine blouse, but no trouble at all to pick up a man's dress shirt and tie somewhere. Did you put it on your credit card? No, you're too smart for that. How'm I doing so far?"

"Not bad for a man blowing smoke out of his ass."

"So you and a bunch of executives dropped by the studio to watch a taping of one of your witless game shows, and being the network's number two, no one would challenge your right to be wandering around backstage, messing around the prop table. Did you have Raymond Sheed picked out ahead of time, or was it a spur-of-the-moment thing? Maybe you saw his wallet sticking out of his jacket pocket in the prop locker. Only a big dumb shit leaves his wallet around where anyone can steal it."

Sanda let a smile, or the shadow of one, flicker across her face for just a moment, and then banished it.

"Then you picked out someone to do your dirty work for you. A street kid, a whore, someone who wouldn't be missed and who was such an ideal victim that his death would hardly be remarked on. Passions run high down on Santa Monica Boulevard. Prostitutes of both sexes get killed all the time, and no one makes much of a fuss about it, not even the police. You cruised the boulevard and found Robbie and told him—what? That you wanted him to run an errand, deliver a package? What was it? Maybe an envelope he was supposed to hand Steven through the car window. Something that would conveniently burn up in the explosion. Very nice. And you got away clean, or thought you did, until that night I came to the car rental office. Jennifer gave me the same dog and pony act she'd given the police, and she did it with such a dazzling smile that my hormones got in the way of my judgment—not the first time, I might add. So I bought it, and asked her for a date, and she was just tantalizingly vague enough that I thought I had a shot at her. Of course, I left her my card, and she showed it to you and you thought it might be a good idea if she did go out with me. So she called and said she was free for dinner that very evening."

"Sanda, make him stop," Jennifer said.

"Not now, Jen, I'm on a roll. I noticed the smell of cigarette smoke the first time I walked in here. I've just quit smoking, so I'm aware of things like that, and then she ran around emptying ashtrays full of lipsticked butts. Later when she told me she didn't smoke I should have remembered that smoke and those butts, but as you so charmingly remarked, Jennifer, all men think with their dicks, and I was much more inter-ested in wooing and winning you than in trying to pin a murder rap on you, so it didn't really register." I turned back to Sanda. "Did you tell her to go to bed with me, too?"

Sanda's back stiffened, and she glanced over at Jennifer but didn't say anything. She was a cool one. No. Not cool. Cold. Like the water on the bottom of the ocean where sightless fish grope their way along the dark sandy floor.

"It was quite a blow to my ego when I couldn't get her

turned on even after we were in bed, naked," I said, enjoying watching the barbs sink in. "I've always thought I was a reasonably capable lover, but I automatically assumed it was me, that I'd done something wrong, or said something, or that my breath was bad. It never occurred to me that I couldn't have turned Jennifer warm with a week's worth of foreplay because she just doesn't respond to men, and that all those hungry kisses and rubs and strokes were just an act. You're a good actress, too, Jennifer. You could have made it in television. You both counted on my bruised ego, didn't you?"

"This is getting boring," Sanda said. "Why don't you go?"

"I want to make sure I have everything straight. When Jennifer showed up in my office to say she wanted to make things up to me, she was really trying to find out, as she had been all along, how much I knew, whether I was getting close, and I was so relieved I hadn't lost my fatal charm after all that I didn't see it, and I was stupid enough to tell her I'd ruled out Robbie Bingham as the intended victim after all. I accepted the fact that she was scared the killer was going to come after his only witness, and I'm a sucker for vulnerable women.

"Except she wasn't the only witness. There was another street kid—Jimmy is his name—and he saw the BMW, he saw the man with the mustache. He didn't take that good a look, and I guess Robbie didn't either. Robbie told his roommate about the guy who was going to kick across a hundred bucks the next morning and didn't even want to have sex. That part never quite fit for me, but it still had me and the cops looking for a male perp." I smiled. "That's police shorthand for perpetrator."

"Don't patronize me, Saxon. We have several cop shows on our schedule."

"Ah yes, your schedule. The schedule that came out of the fertile brain of Sanda Schuyler while Steven Brandon took all the bows and accolades. Was that your motive? Or was it that if Brandon left the network you'd be the logical one to step into the top spot, where you could make sure that your lovely accomplice here got a nice, lucrative career going without having a bunch of dirty old men slobbering over her? What I don't understand is why you couldn't wait. Brandon gets job offers every week. One of these days he'll accept one. Nobody stays put in show business, especially on that high a level."

"Sure he gets offers," Sanda said, her composure cracking just a bit. "But Steven is the supreme egoist. He would have had to name his own successor. And it wouldn't have been me."

"How can you be so sure?"

"It would have been that twit, Irv Pritkin. Steven feels that a hardheaded money guy should be running the show, and that creative types like me are best left one or two rungs down. Irv is a pale carbon copy of Steven." She drew herself up to her full height. In her slippers she wasn't quite as tall as she had been in her office. "Besides, Steven doesn't like women. He fucks them, but he doesn't really like them. And he especially doesn't like dykes."

"And you figured that the job should have been yours by rights, so you had to get rid of him before he had a chance to make what you thought was a bad decision? You were going to be passed over after you'd worked so hard and learned the business so thoroughly. Even engineering and electronics. I guess that's where you learned how to set off a charge of dynamite by remote control." I leaned over and picked up the remote-control unit from the top of Jennifer's television set. "Is this the murder weapon, or did you use your own?"

"You have a marvelous imagination, Saxon," Sanda said. "If you weren't such a dork I'd find a place for you in our story department."

"I don't think so. You didn't want me anywhere near the network. You were still hoping everyone would think it was a homosexual killing, and you figured that Stu Wilson, being a man of volatile temper, would scare me away by threatening me with blackballing. You don't do your homework, Sanda, or you'd know that acting has been little more than a hobby with me for many years, and I don't give a damn if I ever work again. Besides, I had Brandon to protect me.

"But then I told Jennifer I'd narrowed it down enough to know it was Brandon who was the primary target. And you started running scared a little bit, so you tried to kill me with the same dynamite trick. Unfortunately someone else was driving my car—unfortunate for him, poor devil, and unfortunate for you. Because now I knew the killer knew I was getting close, and the only one who could have known that was little Jennifer here, because I was dopey enough to think she was frightened and I told her so she wouldn't be worried."

Sanda stubbed out her cigarette in the ashtray. The brand and the shade of lipstick matched the others. "This is all conjecture on your part."

"Pretty good conjecture, I'd say."

"You arrogant bastard!" She went over to an end table and got a fresh pack of cigarettes from the drawer, making quite a production of opening the package and tapping a cigarette out. "Your problem is that it's *only* conjecture at this point."

"I don't really think so, Sanda. If we stick a mustache on you I'm sure my witness could pick you out of a lineup. And since it was his boyfriend that got killed in my car this morning instead of me, I'm sure he's anxious to talk to the police and help out any way he can."

She reached back into the drawer and pointed a little .22 pistol at me. It was silver-plated. What they call a ladies' gun. "Damn you, Saxon!" she said.

Jennifer gave a little scream, the kind actresses come up with in similar situations on television. It wasn't very convincing.

Sanda said, "The arrogance of the male sex constantly

amazes me. Did you think you could waltz in here with your accusations and then waltz out again? I have no compunction about killing. I was careless this morning, or just unlucky; I won't be again."

"You already have been," I said. "From across the room that gun isn't going to do much damage unless you shoot me right in the heart or in the head."

"That can be arranged."

"But then Lieutenant DiMattia and Sergeant Lawton, who accompanied me here and are out in the hall, would hear the shot and kick in the door."

Her face turned ashen. "You're bluffing, Saxon."

"Fine," I said, "go ahead and shoot. Or would you like to check the hallway first?"

Her hand shook. Guns do that to most people. Unless you've been in a war you don't often find yourself aiming a gun at another human being. She looked at the door at about the same time Joe DiMattia's unmistakable knock rattled it.

"I'm sorry, Sanda. You almost got away with it."

"Bastard!" she screamed, and pulled the trigger.

I was lucky that time. Sanda Schuyler was one of the most knowledgeable and capable women in the television industry—but it seems she'd never learned how to shoot.

The bullet made an insignificant little hole in the plaster on the wall about two feet over my head, and then there was a terrific crash and the door splintered open, and sure enough DiMattia and Lawton came into the room with their weapons at the ready, and this time Jennifer's scream was genuine.

Too bad. She would have made a hell of an actress.

19

On the advice of her attorney, Jennifer London told authorities that she had indeed falsified the papers at the car rental agency, fully aware it was illegal, because, she claimed, Sanda had told her it was important to both their careers. However, she said, she had no idea the car was going to be used to kill anyone, and had she known she never would have dreamed of doing such an awful thing. Later, after the bomb exploded, she said she was too terrified to go to the authorities with her story; terrified of them and terrified of what Sanda Schuyler might do to her. I heard from Ted Lawton that it was an impressive performance. Of course, I wasn't there.

Nor was I present at the Sybil Brand Institute, the Los Angeles prison for women, the next day after Sanda's attorney told her what Jennifer had said and Sanda got hold of Jennifer in the dining room. I'm told it took five female deputies and three hefty trustees to peel the enraged Sanda away from Jennifer's throat. I heard the account from a lady of my acquaintance who is with the sheriff's department at the institute, who wasn't there either but heard it from her friend, who was one of the five deputies.

So the district attorney prepared an indictment of Sanda Schuyler on two counts of first-degree murder—Robbie's and Barry's—two counts of attempted murder—Brandon's and mine—grand theft, auto; the theft of Raymond Sheed's wallet; and several other counts well-calculated to keep the case in court for months and make a media star of the prosecutor. The assistant DA was dissuaded from including a few counts of unnatural sex acts when Sanda's lawyer pointed out he had her dead to rights on the important stuff and would only manage to look like a jag-off trying a convicted murderess for sex between consenting adults. I was told all this by an L.A. *Times* reporter who covers the DA's office. I wasn't there.

The prosecutor also had plans for Jennifer, who agreed to turn state's evidence against Sanda and plead guilty to being an accomplice in the auto theft; and she'd plead innocent to all the changes involving murder because she hadn't known what Sanda was planning to do and never would have cooperated otherwise. It was the old innocent by reason of stupidity defense, and I had no doubt it would work like a charm for Jennifer. Especially after she got through convincing the jury she'd been an innocent young girl seduced and corrupted with promises of stardom by a Deisel dyke, another innocent victim of the casting couch. When her case finally came to trial several months later I *was* there as a prosecution witness, and her lawyer made ka-ka out of my story when he forced me to recount my date with Jennifer and to state I had begun to suspect her when we were in bed and I couldn't turn her on. "I'm sure we all envy your sexual prowess, Mr. Saxon. You're totally irresistible to normal women, aren't you? Best we all lock up our daughters." Jennifer was found guilty and given a suspended sentence, and I added to the imbalance of horses vis-à-vis horses' asses.

But on the second day after Barry Haworth's death, on the day my headache finally went away, I had other things to do, other ends to tie up. Steven Brandon had paid me a handsome bonus, and the network was supplying me with a company car for the next three years, since I had been underinsured on my Fiat when it and Barry Haworth had exploded into pocket-size pieces. I was going to miss that Fiat. I was also going to miss my apartment, since a representative of the building's absentee owners had paid me a visit and suggested very strongly that, to protect the other tenants from future incidents such as the car bombing, it might be advisable for me to make other living arrangements as soon as possible, and that since I had listed my occupation as "actor" when I'd moved in some five years earlier I had lied on my application and was subject to eviction anyway. They told me I had thirty days, which they seemed to feel was damn nice of them and which I felt was totally unreasonable. But I didn't have much choice.

The specific loose end of which I speak was rankling me badly, and since I had a few extra dollars in my pocket courtesy of Steven Brandon, I hired Ray Tucek to accompany me on what I hoped was a final trip to Boys Town. Ray didn't want to accept the money. During the last few days he had grown rather fond of Marvel and was teaching him the finer points of boxing and *hapkido,* and he begged to accompany me for the fun of it, but I always pay my way.

"Let me mess the son of a bitch up, why don't you?" Ray entreated in the car. His car. I didn't have a car yet.

"No, I just want you for backup."

"Just a little bit."

"I've already messed him up myself, twice," I said. "I just want to make sure he doesn't start shooting."

"He won't. He's out on bail."

"Even so."

We parked right in front of the apartment building, and Ray eyed it with distaste. "Falconwood, for Christ's sake," he said. "Never trust anyone who lives in an apartment building with a fancy name."

"Never trust a guy with a tattoo that says 'Mom.'"

"Never trust a restaurant where the specialty of the house is owl."

We went into the building and the banter ceased. I was really feeling tense. Sanda Schuyler had committed a couple of senseless murders and two innocent people had died, but it was my firm conviction that Tony Haselhorst was by far the greater menace to society and was the one that belonged behind bars. I also had a couple of personal scores to settle, and Ray had insisted that I leave my gun at home. He, however, was wearing one under his jacket.

This time there was no need to break into apartment 26, no reason for stealth or guile. This time I just hammered on the door.

To say that Tony Haselhorst was surprised to see us would be to emasculate the word *surprise*. The only thing that kept his jaw from dropping onto his chest was the fact that it was wired shut while the break was setting. He gave a little grunt and backed into the living room. Ray pushed his way in and I followed. Brian was sitting at the kitchen table, looking worried.

"What do you want?" Haselhorst said through his clenched teeth. He sounded like Gary Cooper.

"Is your jaw going to take long to heal, Tony?" I said. "Must be playing hell with your sex life."

Brian stood up, speaking of the devil. "You've got no business here, Saxon," he said.

"Just a convalescent call," I said, "to see how the patient is doing. Oh, and this is Mr. Tucek. He came along, Tony, just in case you thought you were the only one with friends."

"I'll have your ass on assault charges," Tony grunted.

"No, you're not going to have my ass at all, I'm afraid. But speaking of asses, I'm here to tell you to cover yours."

Tony tried to smile, but with a wired-shut jaw it is difficult at best, and for someone who did it so rarely anyway it proved impossible. It came out an Edward G. Robinson–type sneer.

"Why you think they let me go?" he managed to say. "That trick book don't mean fuck-all, and I can beat the rap for possession of a firearm."

"You're right," I said. "But can you beat the rap for pandering? For pimping? For child endangerment? For statutory rape?"

He snorted through his nose. "Prove it."

"I can't," I said. "But there's a young man named Jimmy who's pretty ticked off at you. And another one named Marvel. They are both down at the hall right now singing their hearts out to the city attorney. I suggest you get yourself a good lawyer."

His pasty face became even pastier. "You're bluffing," he said.

"Afraid not," I told him. "Tony, I'd like nothing better than to rebreak your jaw, or to let Ray do it for me. But I don't operate like that. I'm going to let all those nice guys at San Quentin have you first." I turned to Brian. "As for you," I said, "I've sworn out a complaint against you for assault, and Jimmy will back me up. But don't worry, when you get out of prison your seat on the stock exchange will be waiting for you."

Haselhorst took a step toward us, and I said, "Ray, if he moves again, break his nose." Tony retraced that one step. I think the thought of prison frightened him much less than physical pain did. Brian, on the other hand, had not been physically threatened, but when I'd told him he was in trouble with the law his face had turned as pale as Tony's. The two of them were a portrait in terror: cornered rats watching the approach of a battle-scarred tomcat. I must confess here a feeling of great enjoyment. I'm not proud of it, but neither do I deny it.

We left them that way, Ray and I, and were crossing the courtyard with its steaming pool when Brian came running up behind us.

"Mr. Saxon, we have to talk."

"I've got nothing to say until we see each other in court, Brian."

"You can't," he said. "I wouldn't last a day in jail."

Ray said, "If you can't do the time—"

"Please." He put a hand on my shoulder, almost loving, almost caressing. "What would it take to get you to withdraw that complaint against me?"

"Nothing that you've got."

"Look, I told you I do pretty well. I can pay you. How much do you want?"

"Brian," I told him, "life's full of little risks. That's part of the fun. Isn't that why you're a whore?"

The lady named Paula at the Bishop School turned out to have as nice a face as she did a phone voice. She was tallish, with dark hair cut in gentle feathers around her face and gray eyes like the color of a sidewalk. Her smile was warm and genuine and it made me feel good. What she was telling me made me feel even better.

"According to the tests," she was saying, "Marvel has the reading ability of a second-grader. But he has absolutely normal intelligence. He can't read because he was never taught, and his speech problems come from what's commonly called a lazy tongue. We have therapists here at the school who will work with him."

I glanced out the window of her office to where Marvel was playing basketball with some of the Bishop student body. He moved well, had a mean fake, and although not too many of the shots he took went in, they were close enough for someone who had probably never played basketball in his life. He looked like he was having a good time. He looked like a kid.

I said, "He has no brain damage?"

She shook her head. "None that we could find. He's almost like a feral child, a child brought up in the jungle."

"He was, really."

"He seems rather bright once you get through to him," she said. "And he also seems like a rather nice person."

"I think he is. I'm having my troubles getting through to him."

"May I make a suggestion? He's not a hothouse plant, he's a teenage boy. Treat him like one. If you're going to take on this responsibility you can't tiptoe around him all the time."

"He's had it pretty rough," I said.

"All the more reason you should try getting him on a normal routine with normal responsibilities. We're all accountable for our actions, no matter how young or old we are. Marvel is perfectly capable of distinguishing right from wrong. You mustn't pamper him. Just show him affection and understanding, and I'll bet he just blossoms."

"Everyone could use a little affection," I said.

"Exactly."

Paula told me how much the tuition was at the Bishop School, and it made me gulp. But Steven Brandon had done very well by me, and he had also told me that he'd be on the lookout for something I could do in one of the upcoming season's movies, so it didn't seem terribly beyond my means. I signed a contract with only a small flutter of trepidation.

"We'll take things slowly with Marvel for a while, until we find exactly what he's capable of doing," Paula said as we stood on the steps to the school. "We'll try to get him on track as soon as we can. We'll need some help from you, though, Mr. Saxon. I'll want to work fairly closely with you during Marvel's first year."

I smiled down into those sparkly gray eyes. "I think I'd like that," I said.

Her face flushed a rather pretty pink. I just might enjoy this parenting business.

I collected Marvel from under the hoop and we got into my new car, or rather, the car Triangle was supplying me. It was a gold LeBaron convertible, several steps up from the Fiat. It was mine for three years, they had told me, as a special thank-you from the network. I felt good driving it.

"We'll probably move closer to the school at the end of the month, Marvel, so you won't have so far to walk. I already have a real estate person looking into getting us a bigger place."

"Tha's cool," he said. He opened the glove compartment and rummaged through the tapes until he found an Oscar Peterson that he liked. He stuck it into the tape player and the glorious sounds of George Gershwin washed over us—and, because the top was down, everyone else on West Sunset.

"What did you think of the school?" I almost shouted, to make myself heard.

"It's okay. The kids be okay."

"What did you think of Paula? Miss Avery?"

"I know what *you* think of her." He looked over at me and grinned. "Your tongue be hangin' out."

"You're turning into a wise guy already."

"Tha's cool," he said.

I parked in my assigned space in the underground garage, and even though the maintenance people had cleaned it up and washed down the walls and the floor I couldn't quite fight off the queasy feeling I got. It was just as well that I was going to be moving. It was time for a fresh start. Beginnings are what life is all about.

Up in the apartment Marvel headed for the TV set. It was after noon, there were no cartoons, but he seemed to have become very interested in one of the daytime dramas wherein Tracy, married to Mark, was carrying Lance's baby and being blackmailed by Angelica, Lance's stepmother and second wife to Brent. It was good that he was going to be starting school the next day; too much soap opera viewing tended to turn one's brain to farina.

I went into the bedroom to hang up my jacket and stumbled over a pair of sneakers that had been left in the middle of the floor. I yelled out the door, "Damn it, Marvel, get in here and pick up your crap!"

He looked heavenward for divine guidance. "Man . . ." he said with that rising inflection so common to all put-upon adolescents. When he managed to get himself up off the sofa and walk across the living room, the weight of his cross upon his shoulders was evident.

I hung up my jacket and went into the kitchen. It was one of those moments in life that seemed to cry out for a cigarette, but it had been forty-six days and about nineteen hours since my last one and I figured I didn't want to start over again. I could hear Marvel banging around in the bedroom, putting his shoes in the closet. He was probably muttering under his breath about the unfairness of life and how unreasonable some adults were about things like sneakers, and I suppose from where he stood he was right. I was in for a lot of heavy sighs and wounded looks to come, and I can't say I was looking forward to them. But it's one of the things you put up with when you have kids.

I opened the refrigerator. There was a carton of John Courage with icy moisture on the bottles that looked pretty inviting, and I almost reached for one. Then I changed my mind. With a heavy sigh of my own I dished up two servings of chocolate ice cream. I knew it would spoil Marvel's lunch, but what the hell, right?